The QUANTUM LOVE GENE

A Story by
Raymond J. Pilon

To Kalvin
Enjoy the Story
Remember the Message!
Hunab- Ku

Rev. Raymond J. Pilon csc ret.

This book is a Fantasy Sci-Fi and the names, except for historical public figures, are fictional. All the circumstances are fictional.

Copyright 2009 by Raymond J. Pilon, author

ISBN 13 Digit #: 9780976277323
ISBN 10 Digit # 0976277328
WGA Registration # 15551691
Company name at time of registration: Anchor Counseling

Raymond J. Pilon
2906 Sooke Lake Road
Victoria, BC, CANADA V9B 4R6
Email: Raymond@quantumlovegene.com

Dedication

This book is dedicated to Blenda my wonderful wife, partner and best friend. Blenda was my initial editor. Thank you for believing in me. To Angelica for the honor and privilege of delivering your message to all the Spirit Light Beings on this amazing home we call Earth.

Pilon /*The* QUANTUM LOVE GENE

Acknowledgements

This is the fun part, the place where I get to acknowledge and express my appreciation!

Blenda: First and foremost, I acknowledge my dear wonderful wife and partner, friend/editor, Blenda. Without her, it would have been very challenging to finish this project. So, Blenda thank you, thank you from the bottom of my heart. Together we delivered Angelica's message of *The* **Quantum Love Gene** to the world. Thank you for the incredible task master that you are keeping me on track and motivated. Thank you for the excellent marketing, editing, ideas, and the numerous tasks you have performed for this book/movie in the past four years. Thank you for sacrificing your own projects as an incredible writer and placing this project in priority.

Galina Coffey-Lewis, author of *Memories, Musings, and Mystics*. Thank you for reading my book, and your fantastic acknowledgment. You said, "This book would make a great movie and it could be hotter than Avatar."

Nelson Brunanski, author of several mystery books the latest one being *Southern Exposure* who said, "WOW! A great story! I love both the story (movie) and the realization that we are all Spirit Beings. You had a lot of nice interplay with what we know, what science fiction has brought us and how the Pleiadians draw the two together."

Skip Rowland, your expert marketing shared with Blenda was most appreciated. **Sandy Levey-Lunden,** your loving support, recommendations and contacts are genuinely appreciated. **Toni Romano,** retired Out-Reach Director of the Edgar Cayce Institute, thank you for believing in us and for your powerful connections.

David Yablecki for a great website; **Michael James** for Internet support when we began.

Rev. Valerie Shanan for your second round of thoughtful editing.

Esther Hart, deep gratitude for a superb job in the final editing, time lines and layout.

Other people who have given their loving support: Merilee Solberg, Shera Rael, Tasha Campbell, Bev Woodburn, Berthe (Bette) Parent, Denise Rowland, Chris Madsen, Loesje Jacob, Karen Wilcox, Jonathan Pratt, Jan Thirlwall, Lisa Brown, Dwight Whitson, Sy and Cat Silverberg, Jeff Craigen and Christine Craigen.

My deep gratitude for spiritual support goes to my teacher, **Rev. Marilyn Knipp**, to **Drs. Kenn** and **Deborah Gordon, Dr. Ernest Holmes, Rev Michael Beckwith,** to the Metaphysical Community, and to all people who share an open mind.

TABLE OF CONTENTS

Table of Contents

Pilon /*The* QUANTUM LOVE GENE

A Note from the Author

I am probably the last person you would expect to admit to having written a book based on dreams. My wife calls it automatic handwriting. I do not know what that is.

What I do know is that while living in Cahuita, Costa Rica in the spring of 2009, I woke up one morning at about 5:30 am, grabbed a cup of coffee and six small wild bananas and sat down at a small table outside. I had an overwhelming feeling that I should write something. I opened a clip board with writing paper and I picked up my pen. Wow! Mountains of thoughts came pouring out of me as I began to recollect experiences from my dream the night before.

It's funny how this happened. When I sat there to write nothing came to me. When I picked up my pen my dream came back like nothing I had ever experienced before. Thoughts and words came to me that I had never heard before—words like "Pleiades" and "Pleiadians." I could not really hear any voices as in a voice outside of my head. I experienced a flood of memories from the dreams of just a few hours ago as the dream became audible in my head.

The Pleiadian character in my book named Angelica spoke to me in my dreams.

I continued my writing for about six weeks. Every day was the same routine. As the story began to unfold I tried to remain objective, but it was hard to be objective about ideas that seemed impossible.

As a general rule, I pride myself on analyzing information with a critical, sharp mind; discerning truth from lies and distorted sound bites. But now, while writing this story, I had to listen to me, "Spirit Being" Raymond. My intuition told me to write all this without filtering my thoughts which may seem contrary to my own belief system.

After the third day or so, the process started to come more easily. By the second week I began to identify the inner voice of Angelica. She was central to most of my memories. Angelica told me about a young man who would become a central positive force to what Earth was facing.

While asleep I returned to this experience of Angelica talking to me. Returning to the dreams became increasingly easy and consequently I got caught up in the most intriguing bits of information.

I only wish I had remembered more of what I experienced in the dreams. It seems that there is some information I simply do not remember.

I think it's important to say that the focus in these dreams was on the incredible, wonderful fifth dimensional reality—a reality that is ruled by Love and made possible by Universal Laws. As you know, the Mayans and many other leading authorities have predicted this change taking place in December, 2012. Angelica never referred to any particular time or date.

In actual fact, or should I say Truth, it has been so interesting to me as an author to have written about something in the book and then, right before my eyes, see that science has discovered some of the things I wrote about. One incident that really intrigues my wife, and she claims just this alone would make her want to read The Quantum Love Gene is what happened regarding the Black Hole with its whirling disc at its core—the Black Hole that is approaching the middle of our Milky Way Galaxy. In the story I describe how we move through this Black Hole at the time of the Alignment of the Earth, the Sun, the Star cluster Pleiades and the Center of our Galaxy. Back to the subject at hand, my dear wife was taking my book with a much deserved grain of salt until about two weeks after I wrote about this Black Hole. I came across a 2003 report made by Dr. Scott Hyman and his colleagues at the Array telescope at Socorro, New Mexico. Dr. Hyman and his colleagues had detected intelligently directed signals. They believed these signals were what the Mayans had been talking about when they claimed that a "Center" was located at this particular place (the Mayans called it "The Galactic Butterfly"). The Mayans predicted 1,500 years ago that this Center was a passage through to other dimensions.

Also, do you remember that planet discovered by the Kepler satellite in November 2011? Well here is a hair-rising fact. The planet is called Kepler-22b. It is a *habitable* planet with an average temperature of 23c. The real shocker is its location. It is in the Lyra system 600 light years from Earth. This is the original home of the Pleiadians, you know, our ancestors who migrated from there to the Pleiades located 500 light years away. Wow! I wrote this book in spring, 2009.

So the question is, "Why am I so emotional about

an event that hasn't even happened yet?" I don't know the answer. Maybe it is the pain I feel when I experience the suffering of others.

I think it is just fine for you to read this story with a fun-loving skeptical eye and make up your own mind what is fantasy and what is reality, or, might end up becoming reality. After all, I'm just a messenger. As Hemingway once said, "Truth is sometimes stranger than fiction."

The dreams are related in story form. Angelica, the Pleiadian channeling through me, believed that if I received the information in story form it would be easier to make a movie and write a book from the information.

Oh! One last thing: It is very important for me to give credit to Dr. Ernest Holmes who in 1926 wrote the influential Metaphysical book *The Science of Mind.* Dr. Holmes was an amazing healer and teacher who had a major influence helping people all over the world to come out of the darkness and ignorance of fear/separation-based religions. Being trained metaphysically made both the information channeled from the Pleiadians and the writing process easier to assimilate.

The other person it is important for me to give credit to is Rev. Michael Beckwith who is the founder of Agape International in Los Angeles and who was selected as the first metaphysical reverend to attend the United Nations peace conference representing the metaphysical community. Rev. Michael Beckwith has a radio program with Hay House radio called *Awake.* He

A Note from the Author

is adamant that when people awaken they will remember that they are Spiritual Beings having a human experience. Rev. Michael Beckwith passionately believes that there is an unlimited supply for all that we need, that we can live in cooperation, that the order of the cosmos is always in motion and that all is well *now*.

As for the purpose of my story, I end here with the famous slogan of the Centers for Spiritual Living. Their message is, "We are here to help in *Awakening Humanity to its Spiritual Magnificence.*" Remember *Who* and *What* you are.

Hey! It's just an opinion!

All my Relations,

Raymond J. Pilon, BA, Retired Minister CSL, Centers for Spiritual Living.

The Day After

5:30 am

Every day I woke up at my usual time with the sun streaming over the ocean waves. I was in Costa Rica, on the Caribbean side, near a small village called Cahuita. My wife and I were house sitting a very charming little casa a mere fifty meters from the Caribbean Sea.

Every morning at 5.30 am (sunrise) I made a cup of coffee with my trusty French press. I grabbed six tiny wild bananas from the hanging banana stick. (A banana stick is what the locals call a branch of seventy or more four inch bananas.) The banana stick costs me about $2.00 and is delivered every second week by the local grounds keeper. We share it with many species of birds and even with the squirrels.

Every day for forty-one days I had an overwhelming desire to pick up my pen and write. I sat at my outside table overlooking the ocean with pen in hand.

My head suddenly burst with activity. I quickly put the pen down. I could hear my heart beating … rather quickly. But my head was silent. "Wow!" I thought, "This is creepy."

Pilon /*The* QUANTUM LOVE GENE

Dream #1, March 1, 2009
Alien Angelica Appears in Author's Dream Making a Personal Request

0535 hours

Sitting at my little table in the morning, I stared at the pen like it was some kind of key, beckoning and daring me to pick it up. I grabbed the pen firmly. My dreams of the night before came back almost verbatim. I began writing as fast as I could.

"Hello Raymond," says a very gentle voice, a voice very familiar. "This is Angelica, do you remember me?"

"Yes," I say, and a sudden relief sweeps over me.

Angelica continues, "Raymond, I have chosen you to play a very important role in the affairs of Earth. We would like you to be a *messenger*. The message is very important to Earth and all its inhabitants. If we act quickly, Earth and its inhabitants may survive. Raymond, the message will be revealed as the story unfolds. Would you consider being the messenger?"

To answer Angelica affirmatively would require a great leap of faith, but I think, "Heck, I have nothing to lose. After all, this is only a dream."

I decide to take the quantum leap and answer Angelica, "I suppose there is nothing to lose. Go ahead with your story. Later, if I agree with the message you want me to deliver, I will do everything in my power to deliver it to as many people as possible."

3

Angelica responds, "Thank you Raymond. I know you can handle this and I will tell you why we chose you to be the messenger later. So you can understand David, who is the main character, and what the story is about, I will introduce you to David through a second dream."

Dream #2, March 2, 2009
David, Boy Genius,
Hears Voices ... Insane?

5:40 am

Angelica tells me, "Here is an introduction to David's story."

Raymond, David is our hero. He demonstrated very unusual development from birth. When he made eye contact, you could feel his Spirit Light Being in his tiny body looking straight into your soul. You could feel his love energy as he broke out into a wide smile. David was a boy genius and developed at an alarming rate. He was walking at two months, talking in full sentences at four months and reading full sentences from a book by his first birthday.

David absorbed enormous amounts of information very quickly. He would read and retain ninety nine percent of it by simply flipping the pages of a text book (from the University), and at two years old had already developed a photographic memory.

David's parents, Pierre and Margaret Chartrand, were both born in a small town in Saskatchewan, Canada in the same year, 1958. They lost touch after high school and then reconnected at Harvard and got married. When David was two years old, Pierre got a job with the US Military in San Francisco where he was contracted to design luxurious underground shelters.

Pierre and Margaret realized they were blessed with a very gifted child. David showed positive signs of unusual abilities such as telepathy, telekinesis and clairvoyance.

Pierre contacted Dr. Ernest Strong, a former colleague he met while at Harvard and who was Dean of a very unusual school called The Universal Institute for Gifted Children (UIGC). Dr. Strong discovered that David had an IQ of over 300. Pierre decided to home school David because he was only two years old and required the love and nurturing of a family atmosphere. Also, they realized David would have a very difficult time in a public or private school setting. UIGC provided the best Montessori type teachers for tutoring. David graduated from high school at the ripe old age of nine and was admitted to Harvard as the youngest student ever at the age of ten.

David experienced the first major test to his spiritual maturity at age thirteen. David's father broke the sad news to him that his mother had been killed in a head-on car accident where the car exploded and her body burned beyond recognition. For days and months afterwards, David woke up looking wildly about his peaceful bedroom. The genius only child was lost in shock and grief.

As the story begins, we experience David as isolated and tormented by his peers. He throws himself into inventing projects in the basement of his house which his father had helped convert into a well-equipped, research facility. David's only friend is Angelica, the extra-terrestrial friend who visits him in his dreams.

Pierre was very concerned for his son's sanity. He found David in his workshop in the basement. "David," he said, "after dinner we are having a family meeting about 7 pm Would you please come and share with me?"

David was absorbed in a very delicate operation. He did not hear his Dad. Pierre moved around in front of David. David looked up startled and said, "Dad, you scared me. You have that "we need to talk look." David then looked his Dad in the eyes and gave him a disarming smile.

Pierre smiled back and repeated his request. David said, "Okay, Dad. I will be there around 7."

7 pm

They met at the dinner table. Pierre started the conversation by saying "David, I know things have been difficult for you since your mom passed away. Son, it is difficult for me too. I also miss your mother very much. My real concern right now is you, David. I hear you talking to imaginary voices and I'm concerned that you may be going down the same path as your mother. You may remember that your mother also heard voices and as you know the coroner ruled that her fatal car accident was due to a hallucination she was having—she simply didn't see the oncoming car and hit it head-on. Son, the thought of losing both you and your mother is too much for me. So, in view of this, I want to take you to see Dr. Reinhardt—the psychiatrist that your mother worked for. He specializes in neurobiology. I'm sure he can find out what your problem is."

Although sounding sincere and authoritative, Pierre was actually thinking to himself, "My God, I have to be strong so I can convince David. Under no circumstances do I want David to know that the real reason I am requesting him to go see Dr. Reinhardt is because of Dr. Reinhardt's ultimatum to me—the ultimatum that either I bring David to him or suffer the consequences, which in effect means that if I don't bring David he will be in danger. I must not let David know I am being blackmailed."

David looked at his Dad, saw how sincere and worried he looked and so, to please his dad, David agreed with the request. David went with his Dad to visit Dr. Reinhardt at the TRACEN Coast Guard Base located north of San Francisco where Pierre worked at a secret military base.

Dr. Reinhardt was a particularly disturbed and very powerful Illuminati enforcer. He was aware of Margaret's connection with Angelica and the Pleiadians.

At the secret military base Reinhardt interviewed David. His attitude toward David was menacing. He accused David, "So you see visions, hey boy?" Dr. Reinhardt stared down at one of David's drawings and remembered Angelica's face from Margaret's depictions.

Again, Dr. Reinhardt said to David, "So you see visions, hey boy?" Reinhardt looked down at David in contempt and disgust.

David nodded his head nervously.

Reinhardt picked up the pace of his interrogation and said, "David you think people from outer space are teaching you things. Is that it?"

David nodded. Then he shook his head.

Dr. Reinhardt demanded, "Yes? No? Speak up boy!"

David, at age thirteen, was quite intimidated and frightened by this large, powerful man with so much dark energy. David quietly replied, "Just Angelica, Sir."

At this point, Reinhardt stepped up the pace another notch realizing he had the advantage. He shook the drawing of the woman at David, saying, "Your make-believe friend, right here?"

David cried out, "She's not make-believe. She's real ... realer then you!"

Reinhardt didn't give up. He knew he had David on the rails and continued his interrogation. He said to David, "Do you know what schizophrenia is?"

David looked down at the floor, shivering, swallowed hard and answered, "It's what my mother had before she died."

Reinhardt grunted, shook his fist at the young boy and said, "Seeing things that aren't real. That's right. You don't want to end up like your mother ... now, do you?"

David returned home after the interrogation by Dr. Reinhardt and the following day David and his father had a terrible fight. Pierre reprimanded David, "I'm forbidding you to talk about them ... your visions and the dire warnings of this friend Angelica. I won't have you going crazy like your mother."

In response to the reprimand, David shrieked, "I'll show you. I'll show you. She's real. I'll figure out a way for everybody to see her. I know I will! I know I will! You can't shut me up. I know the truth!"

David was left with a gnawing feeling he was not able to shake. He wondered, "Why would my dad want me to see a man as awful as Dr. Rheinhart? It simply does not make sense, and yet I know without a shadow of doubt my dad loves me very much. Oh well, perhaps the answer will be revealed in the coming years. I'll just let it go … better not to disturb my dad."

Dream #3, March 3, 2009
David, A Global Force to be Reckoned

David excelled in everything. At age thirteen, the same age when he was interrogated by Dr. Reinhardt, David graduated with honors with three PhDs from Harvard: in Quantum Physics, Computing and Nano Engineering.

David had already had a huge global impact with a series of inventions that rocked the power structures of the Illuminati. At age twelve, David took the EMP (Electro-magnetic Pulse) weapon from the military complex and engineered it to create an *anti-gravity* vehicle. He also solved the energy crisis by harnessing the sun's radiation via the electro-magnetic grid of the Earth. This served two purposes: global free energy and free energy for the EMP "Flying Cars."

The next year, at age thirteen, David built and flew his own EMP craft—he simply loved the freedom of flying and looking down at the Earth from above.

Globally David became a force to be reckoned with. He revolutionized computers by inventing the Quantum-Nano computer. This computer generation was an evolutionary jump forward. One Nano Computer had the computing power of more than a thousand of the best and fastest main frames of 2012. One year after inventing the Quantum-Nano computer, David invented the first real universal language translator. David called it Anyone. This meant *anyone* could talk with *anyone* in *any* language *anywhere*. This was a major breakthrough in global communications. The language barrier was defeated ... no longer an obstacle in communications.

Needless to say, David was a major pain in the financial world and a threat to those few who controlled ninety-nine percent of the Global economy. Knowing full well that the One Percent Illuminati would try to shut down all his inventions, and probably him too, in a very smart pre-emptive move David posted the engineering specs of all his inventions on the web before the military and governments anywhere could shut them down. Ironically the US Government, including the NSA, was using David's technology.

Each day David was becoming a more imminent threat to the Illuminati and their control over the other ninety-nine percent of the population.

Dream #4: March 4, 2009
Will Raymond Deliver The Message?

5:30 am

Again Angelica appears in my dreams and this time her presence seems so soft and ethereal that I feel as if I am part of another world that is far away and far greater than I ever dreamed of. It is weird. I know I am here present in my body yet my thoughts feel like they are increasingly becoming a part of something greater than me that is pulling me into this thing like a magnet.

Angelica speaks gently to me, "Raymond, now you know a little about David, that he is also in communication with me, and that he is facing danger. It would be very helpful to David as well as to all of Earth's inhabitants if you would agree to be the messenger and deliver the important Pleiadian message to your Earth people—the message that can save mankind from destruction. We would appreciate your help."

"Angelica, why have you chosen me? Who are 'We?' What is the *message*?" I ask.

Angelica replies, "Raymond I know you were born with narcolepsy and somehow this seems to have increased your ability to imagine—particularly in your dreams. Although I know you don't have narcolepsy anymore, you do have an active imagination. Also, you have allowed yourself to be trained in metaphysics and therefore you have a reasonable grasp of the divine intelligence of the universe. For example, you know that love is the most powerful force in the universe. Even more important, you embody the truth about *Who* and *What* you are—that you are a Spirit Light Being having this amazing experience in human form. Raymond, this is why we have chosen you."

To answer question two, Pleiadians represent The Inter Galactic Federation of Planets."

And now I will answer to your third question, what is the message? The message is that all Earth's people get the opportunity to remember and embody the Truth that they are Spiritual Light Beings who have chosen to be in human form. The importance of the message will be revealed as the story unfolds."

Angelica pauses before she concludes, "Of course you have a choice. Raymond, you can choose to be the messenger or you can gracefully decline and simply continue on the path of your amazing journey here on Earth."

Although I can not see Angelica, I can feel her presence and of course hear her voice. Excited by this unusual and seemingly important, rare opportunity, I respond, "Yes! I will be the messenger! I will, however, need your help in remembering the dreams when I am awake."

In shock from the commitment I have made, I take in a deep breath and feel a little light headed. I stare at my pen trying to figure out this strange experience. Am I losing my mind? This is a good time for me to meditate, go inside and remember that I am a Spirit Light Being.

I put the pen down. It felt like the door closed, the dream ended. I closed my eyes and went inside to a place I know so well at the center of my Being. There, I sat in peace, one with the Holy Spirit expressing itself in me, through me and as me. In the background, the sound of the ocean waves crashing against the rocky beach just fifty meters from where I was sitting provided a very soothing rhythm. I drifted to that place of peace I know so well.

The Pleiades in reality... the Pleiades star cluster

The Pleiades have inspired a wealth of mythology and legends: fascinating as these are the reality the star cluster is profoundly more wonderful. Historically, the Pleiades were seen as a group of 'seven' stars – its brightest stars: Alcyone, Atlas, Electra, Maia, Merope, Taygeta and Pleione are visible to the keen naked eye. However modern observations show that this most famous of open clusters is comprised of several hundred stars wreathed in intricately structured nebulosity.

At a distance of about 440 light years from the Earth, the Pleiades are one of the nearest galactic open clusters. The brightest stars in the cluster (Alcyone is magnitude +2.8, and Pleione +5.1) are distributed over about seven light years and although faint to naked sight these stars are from 40 to 1000 times brighter than our Sun. From the Earth the cluster's apparent size is 110 minutes of arc (almost 2°) in the plane of the ecliptic: in comparison, the diameter of a full Moon is about 0.5°.

The cluster has an apparent motion relative to the Earth of an angular rate of just over five seconds of arc per century towards the star lambda Tauri, that is, in a south-easterly direction. Thus the Pleiades takes some 60,000 years to traverse one degree.

The Pleiades exhibits one of the finest and nearest examples of a reflection nebula associated with a cluster of young stars. The nebulosity seen here is light reflected from the particles in an interstellar cloud of cold gas and dust into which the cluster has drifted. The apparent blue colour is due to the preferential scattering of blue light by these tiny interstellar particles and is 'streaky' in structure since the particles have been aligned by the magnetic fields between the stars.

This beautiful image of the Pleiades cluster was produced by David Malin of the Anglo-Australian Observatory and is the copyright of the Anglo-Australian Observatory and the Royal Observatory, Edinburgh. The image is part of the AAO UK Schmidt series: the width is about 100 arc minutes, with the north east in the upper right. It is reproduced with the consent of the AAO. Resource: A high resolution image (113k).

Dream #4, March 4

Kepler-22b -- Comfortably Circling within the Habitable Zone

This diagram compares our own solar system to Kepler-22, a star system containing the first "habitable zone" planet discovered by NASA's Kepler mission. The habitable zone is the sweet spot around a star where temperatures are right for water to exist in its liquid form. Liquid water is essential for life on Earth.

Kepler-22's star is a bit smaller than our sun, so its habitable zone is slightly closer in. The diagram shows an artist's rendering of the planet comfortably orbiting within the habitable zone, similar to where Earth circles the sun. Kepler-22b has a yearly orbit of 289 days. The planet is the smallest known to orbit in the middle of the habitable zone of a sun-like star. It's about 2.4 times the size of Earth.

Image credit: NASA/Ames/JPL-Caltech

Find this article at:

http://www.nasa.gov/mission_pages/kepler/multimedia/images/kepler-22b-diagram.html

6:05 am

Some time passed. I awoke feeling relaxed and centered. I decide to go at it again. I stared at the pen again wondering what magic lay ahead, what would I remember? I summoned my courage and with one motion once again I picked up my pen. I was ready to go and knew I had a mission to complete which I had just begun. Moments after I picked up my pen, I heard Angelica's voice. This time I was prepared to listen.

Angelica says, "Thank you for agreeing to be the messenger. Before we move into the action of the story and what will happen with David and Dr. Reinhardt, I will give you a brief history about the Pleiades, Pleiadians and how we came to know Earth. It is important that you understand why we are here, our powers and how we can help Earth and its inhabitants."

"I agree," I tell Angelica. "I would like to know who you are and where you come from."

In response, Angelica says, "Well to begin, the Lyra system is the original home system of planets for the Pleiades."

The Pleiades' system is located approximately 120 parsecs (500 light years) from Earth behind the Taurus system. The seven planets in the Pleiades systems are called: Alcyone, Merope, Eleno, Taygeta, Sterope, Electra and Maia. I know that is a mouthful, but nevertheless, those are the names of the seven planets in Earth Greek history."

Pleiadian history has it that a little over 26,000 years ago, Pleiadian scout ships were on a mission outside their own solar system when they discovered a beautiful class M planet and decided to name it Earth. Although several of their search vessels discovered the remains of Humanoid fragments on Earth dating back one to three million years, they concluded that over this long period of time the Humanoids had become extinct. They also concluded that there was intelligent life due to the positive energy coming from various Citation pods in the oceans such as dolphins and whales, and, of course, also coming from a whole variety of animals and birds."

The Earth being virgin territory not yet inhabited, the high counsel of Pleiades gave its consent to colonize this beautiful light energy planet in the name of the IFOP, the Intergalactic Federation of Planets."

When the High Council deployed the first group of Pleiadians, this first wave of one hundred thousand colonists from Pleiades arrived on Earth. In time they became known as the Aboriginals. According to Pleiadian archives, they arrived 26,000 years ago simultaneously on every continent of Earth."

This is why today there are Aboriginals living in all the major corridors of Earth. The five major corridors include North and Central America, Russia, China, Australia and New Zealand and South America."

Angelica concluded, "So there you have it, Raymond, the first of the current inhabitants of Earth were Pleiadians. The Pleiadian Light Beings who colonized Earth were in fact thousands of years more advanced than were the previous people of Earth. Of course, the Pleiadians are our ancestors."

(I, Raymond the author, will explain this discrepancy relating to our current advancement in later chapters.)

Responding to Angelica, I remember putting my hand up to stop her from speaking and asking, "Angelica, are you trying to tell me that man's origin is not from Earth, but rather that we are descendants from your home world Pleiades?"

Angelica answers, "Yes Raymond, that's exactly what I'm saying. I know it comes as a shock, but that's the truth."

I sat there with my pen in hand, stunned, not knowing what to make of it. "Well," I decided, "I've come this far, I may as well hear the rest of it."

Angelica continues, "The question is how did the Pleiadians get here? Well, look at it this way. It would take 500 light years (120 parsec) to go from the Pleiades to Earth traveling at the speed of light. And if it took a whole 500 light years to get here, did the Pleiadians place their crew in cryogenic chambers, or did they all live for more than 500 light years? No, the answer is that the Pleiadians came to Earth 26,000 years ago already possessing super powers such as shape shifting, telepathy, telekinesis, flying and many more skills that we enjoy today; but these powers were lost about 11,000 years ago. The Pleiadians also came with language, written word, mathematics, astronomy and philosophy."

"So, if the **Pleiadians** didn't travel here in cryogenic chambers, whatever that is, how did they get here?" I ask Angelica.

"Raymond," Angelica says, "The answer is that they travelled by a combination of worm holes and the power of thought. Their entire journey took less than eight Earth hours to arrive in Earth's orbit."

Angelica continues, "There was a second group that is often referred to as 'The Second Wave.' Twelve thousand years ago our ancestors, the Pleiadians, returned. This time they came in five thousand ships carrying 500,000 Pleiadians from the five star systems of Pleiades. Each star system was represented by a distinct race and they were the Black, White, Red, Brown and Yellow Races."

I think to myself, "This explains why all five major races suddenly appeared on Earth simultaneously in every area of the planet *with* language, math, astronomy and music."

This sets my mind racing and I ask Angelica with anticipation, "Who built the pyramids, Stonehenge, the most intriguing crop circles and many other scientifically unexplainable structures?"

Angelica answers, "The Pleiadians, of course, built these gigantic structures. They built them by using their super powers of shape shifting, telekinesis, lifting and transporting objects by thought."

As if she can read my mind, Angelica goes into a more detailed explanation, "Slowly, over the years, they got too lazy to use their Super Powers and like you Earthlings say, 'If you don't use it, you lose it.' The end result was that the Pleiadians became so forgetful they even began to forget who and what they *truly* are ... Spirit Being Pleiadians with super powers."

Wow! That news really shocks me and I am about ready to wake up out of my dream when Angelica continues to download me with more information. Because I want to hear what she had to say, I settle back into my dream.

Angelica continues to explain, "At about 8000 BC, fear and the desire for power and greed spread across Earth like wild fire. The Pleiadians became even more forgetful. Before they completely lost their memories and got amnesia, they had the foresight to build a flashing beacon of light like a star on top of the pyramids that would shine and let their ancestors from Pleiades know where they were here on Earth. After the second wave, the Pleiadians built their largest pyramid around 9551 BC and named it the Cheops or the Great Pyramid of Giza (Khufu). It has big white luminous structures and sits at the edge of the desert reflecting the blinding light of the sun and when finished the Great Pyramid sat 206 meters above sea level. It's gigantic and they built it with their super levitation powers because science estimates that one stone weighing 2.5 tons was lifted into place every minute.Oh! Because by this time the Pleiadians had to please their dictators, they disguised the intent of the pyramids to be a b_____ _____ _____ r Pleiadian _____ disguise by _____ huge burial _____

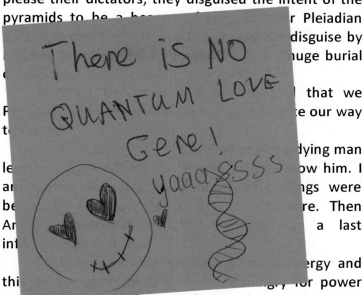

_____ that we

F_____ e our way

t_____

le_____ dying man le_____ ow him. I ar_____ gs were be_____ re. Then Ar_____ a last in_____

_____ rgy and thi_____ _____ for power and the addiction of accumulation. The world was set down a path of wars and self-serving religions. This spawned the most secret and most powerful destructive force on Earth, the Illuminati and they control ninety-nine percent of all the wealth and political power on Earth."

With this, Angelica stops and says, "Raymond, that's enough for now. I will tell you more about us and our history later. Next dream I want to return to David and what happened to him as he continued to threaten the Illuminati."

As I slowly opened my eyes and discovered that my eyes had not been shut, I exclaimed to myself, "My goodness, I thought that I had my eyes closed. Na!"

I laid the pen down feeling mentally exhausted, strangely satisfied and a little disoriented.

Dream #5, March 5, 2009
Strange Happenings

David was eighteen years old. He was very successful in his own business. Unfortunately, because of all of the new incredible inventions that David had given to the world, there was a very high price hanging over his head that interfered with his personal life.

Lately things had been a bit strained at the Chartrand household. David had been called to help an NSA government client. He arrived at the Homeland Security head office, fourteenth floor, where there was trouble with the universal translator software that he invented. David was the only one in his company with security clearance. When David turned on the software program, something very strange happened. A soft-spoken female voice began talking to him in English. "David, be alert! We will contact you soon."

Dumbfounded, David stared at the console. He taped the key to respond, but there is no one there. "I can't believe this," David muttered aloud and yet so quietly no one heard him, "why is someone talking to me ... and how? What's even worse, I know that I know that voice; it sounds hauntingly familiar."

David was very disturbed. After all, he was the world's leading computer genius. David continued with his diagnostics and found absolutely nothing wrong. He thought to himself, "I can't report that nothing is wrong. I must report something. I know, I'll report the following: 'Found minor glitches in sound card

#dl5767, repaired file and rebooted. All is well!'"

Had this occurred only once, David probably would have forgotten about it, but it happened three times over three consecutive evenings. Each time there is no one there, but the same female voice talked to him with words of encouragement. David was more confused and disturbed than encouraged. He knew that he recognized the voice, but couldn't place who it belonged to.

At home David was unable to discuss his work with his dad due to security—top secret stuff. Normally his dad was patient and loving but now David was showing severe signs of distress with unresolved issues surrounding his mother's disappearance. He was told that his mother had died in a car accident but something in his consciousness didn't accept this as true. Pierre talked to David about his distress.

He said to David, "Why don't you go see Dr. Reinhardt? After all, you remember Dr. Reinhardt?"

David repeated his Dad's words in his head. The painful memory of his visit with Dr. Reinhardt flashed into his consciousness and David responded, "Dr. Reinhardt was extremely rude, difficult and very frightening. Dad, how could I possibly forget Dr. Reinhardt?"

Pierre approached David, put his hand on his shoulders, and in a voice filled with frustration, shame, fear and desperation said to David, "I know David, I know."

Listening intently, David could hear in his dad's voice that his dad really loved him.

Dream #5, March 5

Pierre looked deeply into his son's eyes and said, "I really need you to trust me on this one. It will work out."

Inside Pierre was thinking, "It had better work out. Abernathy, who is the second in command of the most powerful organization on Earth, the Illuminati, and Dr. Reinhardt, are both watching my and David's every move. Right now I have to lie to David in order to protect him. I know in my heart the day will come when I can share the real truth with my son."

Dr. Reinhardt was the last person David wanted to see, but to please his father he reluctantly agreed. David said, "Okay, Dad, I will go see Dr. Reinhardt. I will do this for you. Dad, I trust you with my life. Besides, I really want to feel normal again."

Dream #6, March 06, 2009
Corruption at the Psychiatrist's Office

The recalls were getting much easier and the dreams were getting really interesting. I wondered, "Who are these Pleiadians?" I would have to look up the word on the internet to figure out how to even spell the name, Pleiadians. I got my six wild bananas and my cup of coffee and couldn't wait to pick up my pen once again. I surrendered and quickly I lost control over my pen that started writing as if it had a mind of its own.

Special agent Stafford said to Dr. Reinhardt, the psychiatrist, "I'm with NSA. Mr. David Chartrand is a National Security risk. It will be necessary to sedate him heavily and strap him down before you do your doctor thing."

Dr. Reinhardt replied, "Not to worry, I'll give him a dose big enough to knock out an elephant."

Agent Stafford exited just before David arrived at the office.

As David approached the doctor's office, he noticed an unusual number of men in dark blue suits, the government types, loitering in the hallways. At this moment his cell phone rang and the soft familiar voice started speaking, "David, it is Angelica. Please don't hang up. You are in danger. Be careful. We will guide you."

Finally David entered Dr. Reinhardt's office. Immediately he noticed something was bothering Dr. Reinhardt.

Dr. Reinhardt said, "David, I'm going to give you a little sedative to calm you down. Please lay down on the table."

Although David intuitively knew that something was wrong, Angelica's assurance that she would guide him through this terribly uncertain course of events gave David some comfort.

David decided not to let Reinhardt know his suspicions and responded to him in a calm voice, "Okay, Doc, whatever you say. I really want to get back to normal. Things are really stressed out at home. I think my Dad is reaching a meltdown in our relationship. My family means everything to me Doc. So I trust you Doc."

Doc said, "That's good, very good." He rolled up David's sleeve and injected the sedative. David was quickly out of it, well … so it appeared.

Special Agent Stafford returned to the room. As he stared at the table, something weird began to happen. In disbelief Stafford shouted, "Wait! What the hell is this?"

The whole table began to shake and slowly David rose up off the table floating in mid-air. Stafford drew his gun in amazement and fear and demanded, "Doc, I thought you sedated him!"

Doc replied, "I did. I gave David enough sedative to knock out an elephant!"

Right before their eyes David started going

transparent … disappearing like a teleporter on *Star Trek*.

Watching David the Doc said, "Oh! My God! He's disappearing. Look!"

David simply vanished and the table came crashing to the floor; however, not before Stafford and his Military Aide had drawn their guns. They were about to shoot, but something very odd happened. Their guns begin to alter. Yep, they turned into a small handful of metal filings with traces of lead, plastic and the ingredients of gun powder.

Special Agent Stafford was left standing there, his hands cupped together in front of him. He stared down at the little pile of something in the palm of his hand. He stared at the doctor and blurted out, "What in hell is this?" He pointed to his hands. The stress overwhelmed Agent Stafford. He slowly turned around and walked out the door in zombie-like fashion.

What about the Doc? What was happening to him? He was left there dumbfounded, amazed and thinking about seeking help from another psychiatrist.

There was a loud knock on the door. Doc quickly opened the door and two NSA men rushed in.

As for David … well, he was in another world.

Dream #7, March 7, 2009
David's Exotic Flight to Peru

David suddenly found himself hovering above and looking down at the table which had crashed to the floor. He thought, "Wow! This is different."

Next, as though guided by some invisible force, David turned and easily passed through the roof of the clinic. He began to fly away at a tremendous speed out into the cool night air.

David said to himself, "Okay, this is cool, but where am I going?"

The soft, haunting voice of Angelica answered, "Don't worry, David, you are in safe hands."

Stunned and frightened, David asked this soft voice, "Is this the same voice that has contacted me on my computer? Will I come back?"

The voice, said, "David, this is Angelica. You are going to a place in Peru. Of course, you will be back in no time."

David, somewhat annoyed still had a question or two. "Before you take me on this journey, I need to know who you are. I feel like I'm still in my body, and yet I am floating in the air. To say the least, I feel a little strange."

Angelica replied, "I am Pleiadian, and the Pleiadians are your ancestors. I am from a star system known as Pleiades. David, trust your intuition. I know that it is very active and accurate, so when I say to you that I am your friend, I know you will understand. Now enjoy the ride."

David responded, "Okay, so you also read minds. Yes, I do understand … more or less."

Angelica said in a soft nurturing voice, "David, I'm going to leave you now. Later, you will be guided by a lady named Anna. Trust me. You are in good hands."

In what seemed like an instant of time, David found himself flying south along the west coast. As he ascended from what seemed like 6,000 feet to an altitude of approximately 12,000 feet. A moment later he is passing over Marina Del Rey in Los Angeles, California.

Half delighted and half in shock, David muttered to himself, "Yep, I am moving at an incredible speed, over the Panama Canal, and now, suddenly, I am slowing down and descending rapidly. Oh, my God! I'm landing directly in front of a large cave."

Dream #8, March 8, 2009
David's Adventure with the Aliens 26,000 Years Ago

It is strange how one dream seems to blend into the next. I picked up my pen and … .

David was walking through a tunnel. The tunnel was awesome. It was taller than David—about 2.4 meters high and 2 meters wide. The walls were vertical and very black, smooth and shiny. From the preciseness of its design, David concluded that this passage was either man-made or made by some highly intelligent entity. As David inched his way forward through the tunnel, a light emerged in front of him—the light was just like a car light even though there were no visible light fixtures.

In what seemed like the longest ten minutes of his life, David was stuck in this dreadful darkness. The light allowed him to see only about five meters in front of him. He could not help but smell a weird creepy presence—like the lingering smell of an old house empty except for the faint odor of people. Of course, there was no one there. Next David noticed the outline of an elevator-like door to his left. Scared and curious at the same time, David turned toward the door, took one step forward and magically it slid open exceptionally quickly.

David's heart raced, his hands became sweaty and

he thought to himself, "I have to do this; I have to see this through. Besides, I can go back to my bed any time … right?"

With his heart beating rapidly, David stepped forward into a square dark chamber where his thoughts were interrupted by a slight wind created by the door behind him as it quickly closed. A sudden overwhelming feeling of fear gripped him, but it vanished as the door in front of him opened without a sound and he felt the warm air rushing past him. His eyes were suddenly blinded by the bright light of the sun.

David thought to himself, "I am going to quickly scan my thoughts. OK, Where am I? "

As David scanned his surroundings from left to right, and up and down, it hit him that this was a very peaceful, loving environment. In fact, the peace and beauty reminded him of the world-famous Butchart Gardens at Victoria, BC, where a fantastic mini paradise has been built out of an old rock quarry. Anyway, here David was looking out over a beautiful and peaceful Garden of Eden.

David was breathless, and thinking, "Well, after all, maybe I am at the Butchart Gardens!"

As he was daydreaming, his eyes become glued to a new event. "Wow!"

Without any noise, sound or warning, the sky was filled with large weird-looking aircraft. The aircraft looked like very large snails. There were about twenty-five of these vessels. They landed effortlessly without even disturbing the grass. They did not resemble anything on Earth. The entire valley seemed to be covered with this fleet of alien-shaped vessels; they looked like a fleet of snails landing for a secret mission. Each spaceship was the size of five city blocks and about fifty meters high.

David thought to himself, "I should be frightened … right? Something is strangely wrong; yet, quite the opposite seems to be true."

What happened next was nothing short of spectacular.

The ships opened up, ramps were lowered and the aliens come out … a trickle at first.

"Oh! My God!" David exclaimed. Suddenly there emerged a huge crowd of Beings that looked very much like humans. They milled around.

Then like magic, something really weird happened. Something or someone began to materialize right in front of David: first one, then two, then three, then … ten. By the time they all materialized there were ten Beings standing about five meters in front of him. They appeared human, much like our Aboriginals today. David tried to be fearful. "After all," David thought to himself, "I am supposed to be fearful, right?"

Well, these *smiling people*, five adults and five children, exuded what can only be described as *love*.

Watching them David couldn't help saying to himself, "People expressing such loving energy! Maybe they are angels!"

In the midst of his thoughts, David was interrupted by an adult female. She took one step toward David. She smiled, touched an object on her forearm and spoke to David in English.

"Okay," David thought to himself, "This is cool."

The female adult said, "My name is Anna. Please relax. We are peaceful. Tell us your name and where you come from?"

David stood there dumbfounded. He was barely able to speak. He thought, "They seem peaceful—there is no threat like visible weapons. As a matter of fact they are dressed like tourists with their shorts, bright colors and camera equipment of sorts."

David decided to answer their questions, but was a little confused. He said in English, "Sorry I don't speak Alien! My name is David. I'm from San Fransisco, United States of America and my time is 2019. What year is it here? By the looks of your ships I would guess it is way into the future, maybe 2090?"

They all laughed.

"Why are you laughing?" David asked.

Anna responded, "This, David, is 26,000 years *before* your time!"

David felt dizzy, like fainting. He questioned Anna, "Are you serious?"

Anna replied, "David, we are only capable of speaking truth. Is it possible to do otherwise?"

"Oh, my God!" David replied, "You mean you are incapable of lying? Well, that means that I walked through that tunnel and voila! I arrived here 26,000 years in the past. Is that right?"

"Yes," says Anna. "Come with us just for a few minutes. I know you need to get back to your time and space, but first I want to show and explain something to you."

David agreed and they walked together back toward their closest ship called Terra. Anna explained that it was named in honor of this planet.

"That couldn't be," David says. "26,000 years ago, your time, this planet was not named yet."

Again they all laughed. Laughing seemed in abundance here.

"David, you see that tunnel you came through?" Anna asked as she pointed to it. "We built it about three years ago, our time. Besides, David, we have and are visiting your time now."

David gasped, "Oh my lord! I think I'm going to faint. This is all too much!"

David sat down on the grass.

What did the ten Aliens do? They sat down with him on the grass in a semi-circle, and of course they were laughing.

Anna spoke again, "OK, David, here is the scoop. We are Pleiadians from the star system you call Pleiades. It's near or in the Taurus system about 500 light years away from Earth. Speaking in your language, we are Light Beings and we can and do exist in both a three-dimensional world when we choose to take form or in a five-dimensional world when we choose to be in non-corporeal (non-body) form. Because we are in synch, in harmony, with everything, we can do things that you probably haven't dreamed of. For example, David, do you hear the melodious celestial sounds emanating and growing louder and more enchantingly beautiful? The one thousand

Pleiadians below are enjoying themselves so have created this celestial music to harmonize with their enjoyment."

David felt the music vibrate through his body soothing and pampering all his muscles ... in fact, soothing and pampering his entire Being. David surmised, "So this is Paradise. I want it to last forever."

Then as if to show him that having things good is unlimited, these Light Beings started dancing, floating in space harmoniously with the music. Adding to the celestial symphony, the flowers swayed in the harmonic breeze and the doves flew in dance formation in synch with the melody. When all was aglow in the most melodious celestial symphony anyone could ever imagine, the air was lightly laced with stardust."

The stardust was the final touch for David. He reassured himself, "That's it, for sure I am just dreaming. I'll wake up soon."

Anna laughed. It seemed like everyone else was laughing along with her. Anna moved closer and took David's hand in hers. Gently rubbing David's hand, Anna said to David in the softest voice he had ever heard, "David, when you live in integrity, which means in alignment with who you are as Spirit, and you *ascend* to the fifth dimension by your loving thoughts you easily create all the music, all the beauty, all the richness of life that Spirit Beings are endowed with."

David responded by whispering in Anna's ear, "Dream or no dream, Anna, I feel like I want to stay like this forever!"

Feminine Angel that Anna was, she replied, "I

understand David. Your time will come when you can stay forever, but first there is more for you to learn and to do. For example, it is important that you know that the high counsel of the Federation of Planets in our system has approved of our colonization of this beautiful, blue water-filled planet called Earth. Right now we are in this time void of any humanoid life forms. Your visit, David, is an exception. Your visit was ordained and approved. Anyway, we have with us here 10,000,000 Pleiadians who have agreed to colonize every corner of your beautiful globe which is, as you know, another incredible paradise."

Although all this was foreign to what David was taught, the extraordinary experience he was having told him to stay open and receptive to what Anna was telling him.

"David," Anna continued, "in your time we Pleiadians have become known as Aboriginals. We Pleiadians who are present here have no knowledge of your time. When the Pleiadians who are here volunteered for this mission they agreed to take human form which is a real experiment for them. You see, normally they simply choose to remain in their fifth dimensional state of Being. The purpose of this experiment is to see if we can successfully adapt and develop in human form. As you are witnessing, these 10,000,000 Pleiadians from Pleiades possess incredible powers such as telepathy, telekinesis, shape shifting and the ability to alter matter as desired. These gentle Spirit Beings are totally without aggression. They live in harmony with all life forms, all Nature!"

David was sitting there on the grass trying to take in all that had been told to him. "Wow!" he sighed, "Are you saying to me that you Pleiadians are our ancestors? Are you suggesting that in fact we came from your planet called Pleiades and are not evolved from an amoeba, you know, that evolutionary theory?"

"Well, David, those are formidable questions about which there has been much discussion. There are those, even on our advanced planet, who believe that somewhere in the Universe we designed and developed the biological body that you call humans over 400,000 Earth years ago. They believe that when we designed these bodies we purposely endowed them with a very impressive brain and with hands containing five fingers including the opposable thumb. Anyway, David, to answer your questions: (1) Yes, we are your ancestors, (2) Yes, God IS the Universe, Creation Itself, and for your last answer, (3) Yes, Creation is constantly expanding. It is God Intelligence, expressing its self."

David said, "I feel so humbled by all this shared knowledge and the loving hospitality you have shown me."

David looked into Anna's eyes. As their eyes met it was as if their Souls also met and embraced in tender mutual respect and understanding. David lingered in the moment wishing it could last indefinitely.

Anna heard David's thoughts and said, "David, it is my supreme pleasure to be your guide and friend. Now it is time for you to return back home. Remember this trip. Shortly you will be called upon to help form a link, a way your humanoid brothers and sisters can trust us to help them with a most important and delicate uplifting of global consciousness. This is imperative in your time.

David was left wondering what Anna was referring to. She did not answer. She got up and so did everyone else. So, David got up also. He said, "Wait, I have a million questions."

"Questions, David?" Anna said, "You have a very important mission awaiting you. You are endowed as an incredible Spirit Being with superior spiritual knowledge and abilities that humans in your time refer to as genius. David, trust your Intuition, God Consciousness."

Having said this, in peaceful silence Anna walked David back to the portal. Anna gave David a big hug filled with loving energy.

Instinctually knowing his visit had come to an end, David turned toward the doorway. It opened. David turned around to say good bye. There was no one there.

In the far distance David saw the ships and thousands of Beings milling around them.

No one was there at the doorway; however, David did hear a soft, commanding voice speaking to him, "David, God Bless you! May your thoughts create a happy, loving life for it's about to change very soon. The world will depend on you. One more thing, David, when you return home you will find yourself in a slightly strange place where you will meet Angelica and her four sisters face-to-face. We love you!"

David tried to answer and thank these wonderful

Beings. There was no response.

David stared at the door with a smile. He knew his time was up and it had been an honor and privilege to be a part of this alien experience. There were still a million questions lingering in his mind, but he knew for the moment the questions must go unanswered. David turned the knob on the door. It was time to go home.

Finally! Exhausted, barely able to focus, I put the pen down. Wow, that was amazing!

This writing process from the dream the night before was really getting interesting. Angelica's story seemed to be taking shape. I felt almost anxious to get back to the table and bananas and coffee, and of course, my pen.

Dream #9, March 9, 2009
Sandy Travers and Myra,
the Amazing Dolphin

Dr. Sandy Travers is an African-American PhD graduate in Marine biology. She works at the UC Marine biology laboratory. She is 21years old and was raised by loving middle class Americans. Her father is an electrician and her mother is a school teacher. Sandy has a very special relationship with dolphins. She is able to communicate telepathically; however, this has never been revealed to anyone.

Myra is the amazing dolphin who communicates with Sandy telepathically. Sandy loves communicating with the Dolphins, especially Myra who is so intelligent and loving. On this one particular day while Myra was being fed her daily fish quota, she chatted with Sandy. Myra raced to the center of the pool and slapped her tail against the water and then raced back to Sandy chattering in high-pitched sonic bursts. Sandy had a violent reaction. She clutched her head and sank to the pavement thinking, "What is this all about? Oh my, what a reaction. What could Myra possibly be trying to tell me?"

Sandy had visions. One vision was of an enormous Black Hole surrounded by shark teeth. She looked at Myra and said, "Myra, danger? Danger? There is no danger here! Myra look … no sharks, no danger!"

To this, Myra responded angrily to Sandy. Myra turned and slapped her tail on the water once again drenching Sandy. Then Myra swam quickly away distancing herself from Sandy as if expressing her deep frustration in Sandy's inability to understand her warning of impending danger.

Confused by Myra's behavior, Sandy whispered to herself, "What in the world are you trying to tell me Myra?"

Dream #10, March 10, 2009
Back from Peru, David meets Angelica and …

Remember that Anna in Peru had told David he would end up returning to a strange place?

David stepped through the doorway of the tunnel leaving behind him an incredible paradise that existed 26,000 years ago. He awoke and found himself sitting on something very soft. He opened his eyes and behold he was looking down at Vancouver, BC, Canada.

"Where am I?" David asked himself feeling like he was in a daze. "Am I still dreaming? If not, where are the table and Dr. Reinhardt?" Then he began to recognize the shape of his surroundings and he realized, "Oh! No, my God, I'm on top of BC Place stadium in Vancouver."

Thoughts raced through David's mind, "What, who, where am I?"

"Okay, David," David said to himself, "calm down, I'm a cool, calm and collected Spiritual Being. What! Where did that come from?" He closed his eyes, took a deep breath and instinctively he knew what he was about to hear and see would change his life forever, *or*, was it already changed?

"Wow!" David exclaimed to himself.

Struggling with reality, David had a pounding headache; but when he opened his eyes again the reality was so weird he wondered, "Am I still in the dream?"

David noticed the headache had left his mind. "I feel very different," he mused. Then David put on his critical hat and began to examine his situation. First, he remembered the many weird powers like flying effortlessly at incredible speeds. These and many more memories flashed through his very busy mind. Then, suddenly, once again he realized that he was sitting atop the BC Place dome. As David looked around he could see Vancouver from a bird's eye view. David thought, "Now I am cognizant of the fact that I am not a bird nor can I fly. Yet there remains the unexplainable fact that here I am sitting on top of BC Place. How did I get up here?"

"Alright." David asked himself another question, "Is there a relationship between my dream and this situation?" Just as the answer was about to materialize, his thoughts were suddenly interrupted and he wondered if he were strong enough to cope with all the interruptions and strange happenings and the possibility that his life as he once knew it might be gone forever.

A little loving voice inside him spoke to him. It was a familiar voice and seemed like the one he communicated with who called herself Angelica. She seems ready to help.

"David" Angelica said in a soft, soothing voice, "Open your eyes."

David slowly opened his eyes.

Five Women appeared out of nowhere; they just materialized—they simply beamed down.

Watching this, David wondered if he were

hallucinating. He thought, "I must be going nuts." Yet, that little voice inside of David spoke again, this time reassuring him, "David, you are okay. You are quite sane and awake. Remember me? I am Angelica."

Barely finding the energy to respond, David managed to utter, "Yes I remember. You spoke to me through the Universal translator at the NSA computer, and again at the Doc's office."

David was beside himself, teetering between sanity and well, something he couldn't fathom.

Angelica noticed his state of being and said, "Yes, David, that was me. You are very sane David. Remember DR. Reinhardt's office, the table? Remember Peru?"

He managed a slight nod and Angelica continued, "Well David here is the good news. Your Quantum Love Genes will be activated soon. David looked at Angelica and since he was overwhelmed with Love, he concluded this was a good thing. He straightened up and smiled at Angelica.

Angelica continued, "Now David, here is more good news. You are alive, sane and much more. These new genes, well, your Quantum Love Genes, are dormant in you … they are residing in you, but are not yet activated. You know that in human terms you are a top genius, right?"

David nodded and Angelica continued, "David, I am going to give you a sample of what it will be like when your Quantum Love genes are activated. Here goes! You are *ascended.* That's right … you are in the fifth dimension."

David went numb for a full ten seconds trying to take it all in and forced himself to remain calm. He responded, "Did you say ascended?"

Angelica said, "Yes, you are now alive in the fifth dimension. Perhaps I should explain. You see, David, I know that you know intellectually and metaphysically what multiple dimensions are. Although you have not shifted completely to your new fifth dimension, you will very shortly. David, do not worry about your family."

David thought, "It's as though she can read my mind".

Angelica said, "Yes, David, I can read your mind. In time you will read my mind as well. David, while you are in ascended state, in addition to being out of your body you are able to also be in your body as you are now."

Dream #11, March 11, 2009
She Really Knows How to Weave a Story

"David," Angelica continued, "These are my sisters. At my side is Sara from the planet Maia. She represents the White race. Next is Teresa from the Planet Electra and she represents the Red race. Next is Shari from Antelope and she represents the Brown race. Then there is Karen from Merope and she represents the Yellow race. I am Angelica, and I am from Alcona representing the Black race. I am also spokesperson for the Pleiades on this mission. Together we Sisters represent the Intergalactic Federation of Planets."

All five beautiful women bowed slightly. They greeted David with warm smiles and positive energy. They were all dressed similarly in very modest white and pink long gowns. They looked to be about 20-25 years in age. Their poise was regal and demonstrated a definite disposition of confidence supported by an inner power he had never seen before. To David, all five Sisters appeared similar to Angelica in height and head features including their bald heads; however, there was one striking difference: color. Angelica's sisters were White, Brown, Yellow and Red. David exclaimed, "Your sister's distinctive colors are just the same as humans on Earth possess! This is too cool!"

"This is true," Angelica said. While she spoke, Angelica peered into David's eyes searching for mutual spiritual connection. As they looked into each other's eyes loving Light Energy was evident in all its power and magnificence. David felt humbled beyond description. He bowed his head slightly in respect of this highly developed Holy Being. Returning the favor and also bowing slightly in mutual respect, Angelica said, "Remember this David. We are all Spiritual Light Beings. On the planet, Pleiades, we are simply more advanced because Pleiadians on Earth forgot who they were 10,000 years ago. We are your ancestors."

Angelica then motioned with her hand saying, "Come and sit with me and my sisters. We have much to discuss."

Somehow David's feet found the muscles to move. David, Angelica and her sisters sat together in a semi-circle still on top of the stadium.

David mused to himself, "I've got to see the tenuous sanity of this situation. I'm sitting on top of the huge sports dome in Vancouver, Canada with five beautiful female Spiritual Beings from the Star system they call Pleiades. I can't help but conclude, "This is incredible! Either this is super cool or I have lost my marbles and don't care." As he thought this he felt an overwhelming sense of peace and calm wash over him. He looked, I mean really looked at all five women from outer space. The fact is that they looked like any other beautiful women on Earth."

This realization prompted David to ask a question. He said to Angelica, "May I ask you a question?"

Angelica responded with a warm smile, "Please do."

David replied, "OK, thanks," and returned the smile. Then he contorted his face with a questioning frown searching for the right way to ask this delicate question.

While he was still trying to find the right way to ask the question Angelica interrupted his thoughts saying, "David the answer is 'Yes.' Our true natural appearance is somewhat different. Imagine for a moment what people here on Earth might look like say 100,000 years from now?"

Then Angelica paused and David responded, "I see your point."

Angela then continued, "Let me show you, David, what we really look like."

Right before his eyes Angelica began to transform herself. In about five seconds David's eyes connected with almost exactly what he had imagined. There, right before him stood a Being about 5'7" tall and very slender with unusually long arms. Her fingers were long. Her head revealed the most striking change from our present civilization. The face was slim and very beautiful. Her head was larger than our normal size with particular emphasis on the frontal lobe. The back half of the head was also slightly larger and elongated. Angelica's ears were pinned back tight against her head and she was without hair.

"Wow!" David exclaimed, "You are truly magnificent! What's more, I know that you know I am telling my truth straight from my heart."

David smiled again, then he closed his eyes and a few moments later she reappeared as before.

David said, "Thank you!" He then added, "This may come in handy when communicating with our more skeptical Earth Beings"

I'm out of bananas this morning. Oh well, at least I have my coffee and my pen ... .

Dream #12, March 12, 2009
David in Ascended State

Angelica said, "David I need to explain a few things about your *new* self that you will soon change into. I want you to be ready for it, so we are going to give your *new you* a trial run. Now David I know you can handle all this, so I'm going to say it straight out."

David interrupted Angelica saying, "Yes, I think I can handle most of it. That was a great dream. I love to fly in my dreams."

"Well, that's good", Angelica said, "Testing out your *new you,* you will experience in your ascended state that you possess many powers. You can and will learn to use these powers. You are a true Light Being. David, you emanate only love and positive thoughts for good because you operate via Light Loving energy. And David," Angelica continued, "You will master all of these powers in very short order. Furthermore, you will be called upon shortly as a spokesperson for your fellow Earth Beings."

Explaining in more detail Angelica continued, "David, you are a scientist, and you are aware of the scientific body of evidence with respect to the pending end of the 26,000 year Time Line, right?"

David replied, "Yes, I am aware of the coming alignment of our solar system with the center of the Milky Way Galaxy. Most scientists agree that there is also a Black Hole in which a whirling disk of positive light energy will soon manifest; however, they do not agree with the implications this will have for our planet—the consequences. I suspect that many different ideological beliefs couched in various political and religious mind sets cast a very long shadow over the truth. You know that on Earth ninety-nine percent of Earth's economic, political and military power is held by less than one percent of our total population? I'm sure that this news comes as no surprise to you ... that it's actually a much smaller number, or should I say Organization, which holds the purse strings ... that controls the power."

Angelica was impressed and replied, "Yes, that about sums it all up."

I think I am beginning to recognize Angelica's voice, it is absolutely captivating.

Dream #13, March 13, 2009
Creative Balance

Angelica started telling David how things are from her perspective. "Perhaps this is a good time to bring you up to speed on a much larger scale. David, it is important for you to understand that the Universe remains intact. Creation (Hunab Ku) is expressing itself as the universe. It is continually creating balance between the positive Love use of Energy and the negative destructive use of Energy.

Angelica continued, "On Earth, there is a dark force—they are the Illuminati and they are led by a very bad dictator called Roughchild. His ancestors came to planet Earth about 10,000 years ago. This was about the time our people had forgotten who they were and where they came from. Back 10,000 years ago, he was called Vandor and he took advantage of the Earth Being's confusion. With the promise of power and wealth, Vandor corrupted the leaders and instilled the root of all wars—*fear*. The Illuminati are the embodiment of this dark fear-based destructive use of the Force/Universal God Energy. Ever since the Illuminati came into power, fear has dominated the decision-making process on Earth."

Fascinated by the history of our Earth, I longed to hear more. It was as if Angelica were reading my mind and my requests. I lifted up my pen and once again it started its magic for me.

Pilon /*The* QUANTUM LOVE GENE

Dream #14, March 14, 2009
Pyramids and Mysterious
Rock Formations

"Now I will shed some light regarding the big mysteries you are puzzled about," said Angelica. "I know you have been wondering who or what built all the great structures on Earth, such as all the big pyramids and rock formations? The answer is we did about 12,000 years ago. They were built as beacons so our Pleiadian navigators could detect a specific landing site on Earth from a distance of several light years in space. Without going into a lot of astronomical data, let's just say that we discovered levitation or anti-gravity and telekinesis some 80,000 Earth years ago. That is what made it possible to lift the massive stones which built the pyramid of Cheops, the even bigger pyramid in Central America and also the many strange rock formations in many parts of the world. Unfortunately, by 8,000 BC it was all but a mythology."

Reading my mind and knowing I still had more questions regarding the meaning of the rock formations for us and what the Pleiadians wanted, once again Angelica answered my questions through my pen.

Dream #15, March 15, 2009
Many Civilizations

Curious, David asked Angelica, "What does this mean to humans and all life on planet Earth?

"Good question," Angelica replied. "In answer to your question, David, we have been in contact with several people on Earth for a long time. In a recent review of the pending situation, these several people have invited us and our ships to come to Earth in the hope that we may be of some help. I want to be perfectly clear so you fully understand that this help is not imposed, rather help is *offered.* It is up to the people of Earth to decide their fate."

"Okay," David replied. "I get your message—you have come to Earth as invited quests to help out. But what exactly are you and your Pleiadian friends helping us to do?"

Angelica responded, "You see, David, historically there is an event that occurs every 26,000 years, that is, every 26,000 Earth years all these celestial bodies come into alignment with the center of the galaxy. The truth is that the human colonization of Earth has been attempted thousands of times by many Beings from all over this Galaxy. These colonizations have lasted two to ten thousand years. Civilizations end abruptly with major upheavals of the Earth's crust and of course the effects of the 26,000 unit time line scenario. David, these civilizations have simply disappeared with the only trace of their existence being a few bones."

This time we Pleiadians believe the outcome can be different. We believe that Spirit Beings here on Earth have advanced to a point that with a little help from us life on Earth will survive. Why do we care or want to help? The answer is very simple. As I have said before, we are your ancestors. That's right! We are your ancestors! Of course, we won't do anything unless it is the will of your people. Earth people will have to decide for themselves if they want life on their planet Earth to survive."

"Also," Angelica continued her dialogue, "this time the situation is a little different. Earth is experiencing the result of global warming and severe climate changes. The dark energy here, as expressed via the Illuminati, has infected Mother Earth ... behavior such as evidenced by very bad stewardship of Mother Earth.

I was thinking about global warming and other weird climate patterns. As if being sucked into a dream, Angelica continued telling me of events to come.

Dream #16, March 16, 2009, Cataclysmic Events and Climate Change

"As you know," said Angelica, "in the past three years alone, more than one billion people have died from a variety of disasters ranging from massive flooding in China, Canada, Europe and the USA all the way to massive earthquakes on the St Andreas Fault which eliminated Los Angeles and California all the way up to San Francisco. Also, Japan, Peru and Costa Rica were destroyed by a three hundred meter tsunami. Global climate change has had a very significant impact on global political and economic stabilization, or should I say *de-stabilization.* It has in fact brought the world to the brink of all-out war."

"But all of this, David, is nothing," Angelica warned, "compared to what's coming in the next few days. Remember the phrase global warming? Well, most scientists have agreed that as of 2009 if the Earth warmed up another two degrees this planet would lose more than fifty percent of its people. Why? This would happen because with the temperature rising another two degrees, the ice in the poles would almost disappear. Given that sixty percent of Earth's population lives within thirty-two miles from the ocean, and that the ocean will rise about ten to twenty meters, guess what will happen?"

David considered what Angelica was saying and

then whispered, "It is almost inconceivable—50 percent of life on Earth gone. Bingo! Now I know. This is why you are here, to prevent this catastrophe."

Angelica responded, "David, despite all this we have some very good news. We have the ability to completely re-terraform any planet. We can bring Earth and all life on Earth safely through this potentially destructive phenomenon that is about to unfold. Earth would not only emerge through the potential destruction safe, but as a gift to Earth's children you would once again experience the awesome beauty of what Earth was like 2,000 years ago."

A little different, but perhaps a rather pleasant change, you would no longer need highways as you would enjoy the benefit of EMP (electro-magnetic-pulse) vehicles, i.e., anti-gravity machines. EMP vehicles include cars that are powered by the earth's electromagnetic fields which surround the globe. The rivers, lakes and the oceans would be free of pollution and abound with fish."

Once again, David, I need to remind you that whether or not we do this is up to the will of the people living on Earth. We Pleiadians will not impose our will upon you, even though you are our descendants."

David was numb, awestruck with so much information of incredible changes. He had never felt so excited and scared at the same time. With a shaky voice, David asked, "Is all this really happening … am I hallucinating or dreaming?"

Angelica walked over to David, gently took his hand in hers and softly reassured him, "David, feel my hand, look around, open your ears and eyes and smell the city below."

David looked around and with his newly heightened senses became aware of familiar city sounds, smells ... and in the distance he even detected a familiar building—the Sears Tower. David took a deep breath and straightened himself up. He then focused on Angelica and sighed, "Thank you," and squeezed Angelica's hand.

Angelica moved closer to David and gave him a big, warm, loving hug. David wrapped his arms around Angelica and as they embraced David felt a powerful wave of positive loving energy sweep through his body. Attracted by the loving energy of David and Angelica, the other four women surround then and together they become one single-minded group. David experienced a group hug that seemed even more powerful. It was filled with compassion, vision and a keen awareness of the power of cooperating together.

David was filled with an instant insight: Assuming that a majority of the human population expressed a desire to accept their help, which would be indicated by this majority *waking up* and embracing the Truth of *who* and *what* they are—that is, Spiritual Beings having this amazing journey *in* human form but *not* of *it*—then David and Angelica and her sisters would save Earth and its Spiritual Beings, Pleiadian descendants.

Somewhat overwhelmed by his sudden insight, warm tears of joy streamed down David's face. The tears etched David's cheeks with hot burning rivulets of release and excitement. For a moment David held on tight, afraid that if he opened his eyes the magnificent moment might come to a crashing end and once again he would find himself strapped to the table staring up at Dr. Reinhardt.

Reading David's thoughts, Angelica said to him, "David, I'm going to teleport you back to your home in San Fransisco It is time that you seek out the truth about your mother. We will meet again aboard the Starship Cosmos very shortly.

The plot thickens. I find myself quite absorbed with this storyline, anticipating the next stream. Just as I am thinking, "Now is that weird or what?", Angelica interrupts my thoughts and says to me, "Hi Raymond, it is good to see you again, this is the 16th dream and I must say, it seems like you are doing quite well transcribing this on paper."

Dream #17, March 17, 2009
Angelica Takes David
Back to His Mother Issues

David was twenty-two years old and beginning to have some doubts about Dr. Reinhardt's ethics and his involvement with his mother. Something was just not right about the story of her accident. He couldn't put his finger on it, but he knew something was really wrong with that crash story. Based on a hunch and his intuition David hacked into Dr. Reinhardt's medical files. He stared at the monitor with absolute disbelief. Flabbergasted, he heard his heart pounding.

In the files, David discovered wonderful news about his mother. His mother was still alive and confined to room 314 in a local mental institution with the diagnosis of acute schizophrenia.

"My God" David thought, "would Dr. Reinhardt actually commit my mother to an institution for schizophrenia and convince me to believe she died in a car crash. Would he really do such a thing?"

David felt a big knot growing in his stomach and knew the truth, "Rheinhart lied to me. My beloved, innocent mother has been in an institution on a false diagnosis of schizophrenia ... locked up and imprisoned for years. What an unbelievably cruel thing to do to another person! What an evil man!"

David suddenly remembered Sandy Travers, the Dolphin lady he met at the news conference a short time ago. He and Sandy had dated a few times and had a wonderful time. Thinking about Sandy, David wondered for a moment if his relationship with Sandy was developing into more than just a friendship? He dialed Sandy's phone number.

"Hello," said Sandy.

"Hello Sandy," replied David.

"It's good to hear your voice," said Sandy.

David said "It is good to talk with you again." David paused for a moment to clear his throat, and then said, "Sandy, we need to meet. There is something very important that I want to discuss with you. Can we meet perhaps at the Marine Lab?"

Sandy quickly replied, "Of course, David. How about eight o'clock? Does that work for you?"

David responded, "Yes, that would be great! I'll see you then."

They met in the Marine lab in Sandy's private office. David told Sandy about the files, looked Sandy deep in the eyes and said, "I have to confess, I think I may be going crazy."

Sandy stared back at David in disbelief.

David interrupted before Sandy could respond exclaiming, "No, I'm serious! I see visions, maybe even hallucinations, some sort of Gateway opening for mankind, something about a Black Hole and the end of the world. Heck, I might even have visions of the Dolphins."

Sandy broke into a big smile, looked straight into the depth of David's eyes, and took hold of his hands as she said to him, "David, this is the same message the

Dolphins have been giving me."

"Are you kidding?" asked David. "That is absolutely incredible."

David sighed. Then with hot tears rolling down his cheeks, David looked intently into Sandy's eyes and said, "I think we should check out the mental institution where my mother resides. I just can't believe she's alive after all these years. Wouldn't that be incredible—actually seeing my mother again?"

Sandy raised her hand, gently wiped off one of the big tears rolling down David's cheeks and, "Yes, a thousand times yes. We will go find your mother." Sandy gave David a big hug with her arms embracing him a little longer and more tenderly than a friendship hug.

David and Sandy agreed that they would find a way to gain entrance to the mental institution without Reinhardt being aware. To this end, David found and duplicated his father's military ID. To make Sandy's ID, David placed Sandy's image and thumb scan on a new card. He then created a new label that read: Dr. S Travers. Using their phony IDs, David and Sandy gained entry to the mental institution and the isolation room where David's mother was being held. They took the stairs up to the third level in an effort not to be noticed in the hallways. Gingerly, with great caution, they opened the door and peered down the hallway. The coast was clear. Quickly and quietly David and Sandy snuck down the hallway to room 314.

David and Sandy were keenly aware that a moment of truth awaited them. Scared and excited at the same time, David knocked on the door marked 314. What seemed like forever suddenly ended as the door was opened.

There standing in the room was a beautiful woman of about age fifty, David's mother. Margaret stared at the young man in front of her. For a full ten seconds they simply stared at one another ... stunned and frozen to the spot. Then, David and his mother rushed toward each other with arms outstretched and embraced with such a vigorous hug that the passion almost knocked Sandy over.

Overcome with emotion, David's mother started crying, "Oh my God! David, is it really you?"

David was not able to hold back his tears either. He looked at his mother and exclaimed, "Mom, you're alive, but what about the accident? You're supposed to be dead. And yet I found you here. What's going on, Mom?"

In response, Margaret invited David and Sandy to sit at the small table in her room. Holding her son's hands across the table, Margaret said in a very soft gentle voice, "David, I've been expecting you. You see, David, although you could not communicate with me, Angelica has been my eyes and ears into your life all these many years. I know all about you and am so proud of the man you have become."

David just couldn't wait anymore. He interrupted and said, "But why, why didn't Angelica tell me?"

"David, my son, Angelica could not tell you I was alive and sane because it was too dangerous. You see David, Reinhardt knows about Angelica and the

Pleiadians. My beloved son, you had to discover all this on your own … as well as discovering *who* and *what* you are."

David grabbed his mother's hands more tightly and with desperation in his voice asked his mother, "I must know if you know. Please tell me *what* am I?"

Margaret, in full clarity and also glancing at Sandy, said to David, "Genetically speaking, you are Pleiadian as are all people on this planet. David, in actual fact, we are all descendants of the Pleiadians and that includes you, Sandy. You see, David, a telepathic link exists that joins me with Angelica and every Pleiadian throughout the space time continuum on Earth. This Pleiadian telepathic bond is awakened when the dormant Quantum Love Gene is activated in the DNA helix by direct contact with another awakened being. In your case, David, you will be the first Earthling to have your Quantum Love Gene activated. You will be awakened shortly and your Quantum Love Gene will be activated soon."

"All this is hard to believe," said David.

His mother replied, "I understand, but now let's get back to the question at hand. David, this is why Dr. Reinhardt and his elitist secret organization, the Illuminati, took me from you before you reached puberty. You see, Dr. Reinhardt and Abernathy (the Illuminati Boss) concocted the phony accident and locked me up here and forced your dad to lie to you. Abernathy, who is a very evil man, told your dad that if he didn't build a spaceship underground for the elite one percent to survive the pending disaster, he would kill me and you and I suspect many others. David, I couldn't risk your life and not seeing you grow up through the eyes of Angelica. You see, I have always known in my heart that you are in this world for a very special purpose. Soon you will be activating your Quantum Love Gene. My son, I trust you know that you are very special. David, it is important that you go to the Marine Lab as soon as possible with Sandy. At the marine lab you will begin a new transformation of human consciousness."

Catching her breath and speaking rapidly, Margaret continued, "Now, both of you must go quickly before you are discovered. Take the stairs, and there's a back door. This way you will go unnoticed. Don't worry about me. We will be united very shortly."

Margaret got up followed by David and Sandy. Together they shared a group hug. Then Margaret broke from the hug and went to open the door.

Before Margaret had time to open the door, it burst open and eight soldiers with automatic weapons rushed in. David kept hold of his mother's hands desperately trying to save her. One of the soldiers pushed David aside and slammed his gun butt against Margaret's temple. Margaret screamed in pain as she fell to the floor in a pool of her own blood.

David yelled, "No, God. No! Why? She is no threat to you. She is a defenseless old woman."

Before David could finish his outburst, two soldiers pinned him to the floor with their boots on his out-stretched arms. Straining to see his Mother lying very still in a pool of her own blood, David was suddenly startled beyond words. A very bright light enveloped his mom's body. A moment later the light disappeared and his mom's body simply vanished. Her blood stained clothes remained on the floor where she fell. Dr. Reinhardt was facing David and did not see his mother disappear.

Meanwhile Sandy struggled hopelessly to break loose from two soldiers who had her pinned down. Helpless, Sandy had watched the horrible violence unfold. As she saw Margaret's body vanish, Sandy held her breath in an effort to hide the joy inside her Soul.

Just as Sandy thought things could not possibly get worse Dr. Reinhardt, with an attitude of superiority, waved a hypodermic syringe at David. "Hold him down," he yelled at the soldiers. Reinhardt knelt down next to David and whispered in his ear, "David you will not remember this. Reinhardt jabbed David hard with the syringe.

The chemicals emanating from the syringe took immediate effect. David experienced the room spinning as he fell to the floor loosing unconscious, but not before he saw and heard Reinhardt talking on the phone. He heard Reinhardt say to his dad, "Pierre, even if his mother could, I don't think she had the time to activate his Quantum Love Gene and all those extraterrestrial powers. Hell, Pierre, David will not remember any of this."

David focused on his powers. He managed to contact Angelica. "Angelica, I need your help. I am being drugged by Reinhardt."

Angelica responded immediately. "Don't worry,

David, you will remember me. David we will meet you
again, aboard our Starship Cosmos. Very shortly."

About three minutes later David came to with a
massive head ache. He looked up and saw the loving
eyes of Sandy as she held his head up off the floor. He
looked around the room and quickly remembered the
horrible event that had killed his mom,.

Sandy asked, "Can you get up?"

David said. "Yes, we better get out of here before
the security staff find us at this crime scene. He
scrambled to his feet, glanced over to where his mom
had ascended. A smile emerged for a moment, then he
reached over and picked up the dress she had left
behind. He looked up at Sandy and said, "Lets get out
of this night mare."

They rushed out of the Institute undetected. On the
street David said, "I need to meet with Angelica and her
sisters so we can devise a plan to save us all from
ourselves and the Black Hole. Sandy thank you for
being there for me." They kissed passionately.

Dream #18, March 18, 2009
The Plan

David contacted Angelica again and said, "I'm ready to board the Cosmos."

Angelica replied, "We will now teleport you to our mother ship Starship Cosmos.

To the ship controller Angelica said, "One to transport!"

A moment later David was aboard an amazing spacious ship. David and the four Pleiadian sisters devised a plan to awaken humanity and save everyone from destruction from the Black Hole.

Inside of Starship Cosmos, David observed a large lounge-like setting. Through a very big window he could see Canada.

David began a dialogue with Angelica and her four sisters about how they were going to help save the Spiritual Beings (humans/Pleiadians) here on Earth from the certain destruction of their Planet Earth and all life. They decided that they would approach the world leaders of all nations with their intentions.

Although in theory this sounded like a good plan, David was having doubts of their ability to execute the enormous task they had decided to undertake. Coming to his rescue, Angelica decided to explain her and her sisters' abilities, powers and other unique talents. She explained how she and her sisters can use telekinesis, telepathy, shape shifting, time travel and other superpowers more developed than those known on

Earth.

Angelica, as spokesperson for the five Pleiadian women, described their unique talents, "Remember we have many years of development over Earth Spirit Beings. Let's be clear, when we came here 12,000 years ago in the second wave of immigration from Pleiades, we had most of these powers. As I have already said, by 8000 BC, however, our people had forgotten most of their powers. You do understand, don't you David, that our six senses are incredibly advanced?"

David nodded his head indicating that he did understand.

As if she wanted to make sure David really understood, Angelica continued, "Let me show you what I mean. I'm looking over there at the Second Narrows Bridge about 2,000 meters away, that is way far in the distance, and traffic has come to a standstill. On the ramp there is a city bus. Do you see the bus David?"

David looked over to the bridge ramp. "My God," he said, "I can see it. Wow! That is so cool ... like having X-Ray vision."

Angelica said, "Now I will focus on the license plate. There it is. It reads VL7 EE1."

David tried to focus on the plate and couldn't make out the lettering. He said to Angelica, "I can see lettering but it is all a blur."

Angelica placed her soft hand on David's shoulder and softly replied, "That is okay, David. In a very short time you will be able to see as well as I do. My sisters and I have the ability to look at any object, focus on the molecular structure and change it to whatever we want. Soon you will be able to do this as well."

"I can't wait until I have these super powers," David told Angelica.

"That's good," said Angelica, "because there is still more we can do so listen carefully. We can do more exciting things. We can see and hear any frequency on the sound and light spectrums, use our eyes to focus the sun's rays and emit two beams of energy powerful enough to make a hole one meter in diameter and one hundred meters deep in less than thirty seconds and fly faster than the speed of light. Also, using our ships, we can create worm holes and travel through them to very far away worlds many galaxies from Pleiades. Using our highly developed thoughts, we have traveled to Earth in less than ten Earth hours … with our ships, of course. You see, David, our bodies are genetically engineered to be impervious to any known matter or light. We possess more talents, but I think that's enough for now. Right, David?"

"That is right," David agreed. "It sounds so incredible it is almost too good to be true."

"Well, things will change shortly, David," Angelica said. "Soon your powers will be similar to ours."

"Wow!" David exclaimed. With shaky legs David sank into a comfortable chair that quietly and quickly adjusted itself to his body.

"Now let us switch to seeing how we as a team will be using our powers," Angelica said.

"With our powers we will be helping you, David, to deliver the message you agreed to deliver to the people of Earth. This message is that all Earth's people get the opportunity to remember and embody the Truth that they are Spiritual Light Beings who have chosen to be in human form and who are enjoying an amazing experience on this Planet."

We agree to save this beautiful blue water-filled jewel that is Earth from certain destruction from the Black Hole at the same time we help humanity to awaken to the truth of *Who* and *What* they truly are: Spirit Beings, Non Corporeal, incarnated *into* a human body. You are *in* the body but not *of* it. It is our proposal to you that when you accept and embody this truth, we will be able to help you. Yes, upon your acceptance, something absolutely wonderful will happen. Your Pleiadian Quantum Love Gene that has been dormant for 10,000 years will be activated!"

This means that you will ascend to the fourth and fifth dimensions possessing the same powers as your ancestors from Pleiades ... powers beyond your imagination. It's very important here to understand that it is the *positive use of energy* (God-Creation) we are talking about. We call this Love. Love is the most powerful force in the Universe."

It also means that your acceptance and new powers coupled with the protective shield from our 10,000 ships which are surrounding Earth will enable all life on Earth to pass through the Black Hole unharmed. But, and it's a big but, the majority of your people must vote to accept our help. It's up to you, all of you."

"That sounds like fun. I'm willing," David assured Angelica.

"Well, then so be it. This is what you do," replied Angelica. "You discipline your thoughts by thinking only of thoughts that will attract to you the Loving experiences you desire. There is an invisible but nevertheless unfailing Universal Law of Attraction that will respond to your thoughts. You will attract to you exactly and only what you are thinking. As those Southerners in the USA say in one of their favorite expressions, 'You simply think things into existence.'"

Angelica then concluded, "Okay, in practical terms, this is the plan. We will have a vote up in our Starship Cosmos whereupon 13,000 members of the Earth's delegation will cast their vote on whether or not to accept our help."

David pondered deeply about what Angelica had told him and wondered aloud, "Thinking about these billions of people that the 13,000 delegates represent, how in the world can we accomplish this seemingly impossible task? How can we get the leaders to listen?"

"David," Angelica interjected, "my friend, please remember we are the Light. Pleiadians think and act only in a positive constructive loving way. We know what you are saying, or should we say 'are thinking.' This is good. Because at the moment the Dark Energy dominates this planet, you may want us to intervene. David, I know you understand that we have the power to do just about anything we want. And you also know our Truth: that we are absolutely loyal to the prime directive of our galaxy. This directive states clearly that we are never to interfere or impose our wishes and desires on peoples of another planet. Even though you are our descendants and a long length of time has transpired since the Dark Energy started penetrating your affairs, the High Counsel of the United Federation of Planets has declared that its prime directive definitely applies here. The conclusion, David, is that we must decree by an actual vote that it is the will of Earth's people that we interfere."

As they continued talking, Angelica and her sisters decided that each race (as in color) as represented by the five Pleiadian women, would meet with their respective world leaders. Angelica, the black Pleiadian leader, would meet with leaders in Africa and India; the white Pleiadian, Sara, would meet with the Europeans; the yellow Pleiadian would meet with the leaders in Asia (mainly China), the red Pleiadian would meet with the Aboriginal people represented from around the world, and the Brown skinned Pleiadian would meet with the Polynesian people from around the world. David would meet with the leaders of all of North America as his homeland, Canada. Each of these Pleiadian Superwomen would assemble a team and each team would meet via video conferencing.

The technology to make this happen would be provided by several of the Pleiadian ships already in orbit. Every country, every sovereign state, would meet with one or more Pleiadian representatives. The agenda of these meetings would be to inform Earth Beings of the purpose and intentions of these Pleiadian

SuperBeings as it pertains to the Global shifts about to take place—the shifts as our solar system approaches alignment with the Black Hole.

Encouraging David, Angelica said, "If we need more Beings like us to make this happen, we can have thousands here in a flash! Further," she emphasized, "here on Earth the people of the Metaphysical community by virtue of being awakened Spiritual Beings will be a tremendous help. They have the advantage of remembering who and what they are— Spiritual Non-Physical Beings. Although very few of these Metaphysicians know they are Pleiadian, we still have an advantage. You see, David, we have been monitoring Earth's events for hundreds of years. Remember: we are your ancestors. Even though we look different from you, we are *not* aliens, we are Pleiadian ... and in actual fact *all* of Earth's Spirit Beings are Pleiadian. As your ancestors, we are ready to assist your transition to a wonderful new world."

"I get the message," David told Angelica.

"That is very good," Angelica replied enthusiastically and then added, "David, I just can't emphasize enough that even though it is our strong desire to help, it's up to the people of Earth to make this decision regarding whether or not they want our help. It is not the decision of the Pleiadians. I believe one of your famous quotes here on earth is, 'You can lead a horse to water, but you cannot make him drink.' The same thing applies here ... we can offer our help, but Earth's people must be willing to accept it."

Sitting here with my bananas and my coffee, I read over my notes and realize with astonishment who I am. I am Pleiadian. I am inspired and ready for my fourth pen to guide me into action.

Dream #19, March 19, 2009
The Illuminati, the "Bad Guys"

Angelica had said that the Illuminati, the "Bad Guys" number 7,000,000 people—less than one percent of the global population. Keeping this in mind, Angelica said to her four Pleiadian sisters, "We will encounter considerable resistance from the Illuminati. This resistance is very illusive because the Illuminati are the establishment. Anyone who questions the actual existence of this not-so-secret institution puts themselves at risk of being accused of supporting a conspiracy theory. Hidden beneath this fear is the harsh reality that the Illuminati are Earth's Dark Energy—a conspiracy of Global proportion.

"I know about the Illuminati," David replied, "but am wondering how on Earth the Illuminati got started and what the implications are for our Earth people?"

Angelica explained, "The Illuminati, as the word suggests, means 'the light.' Its origin is not clear. Some say it was started seven thousand years ago by a few well intentioned philosophers with the very noble ideal that it is the right of every citizen to be free and prosperous. This ideal was enshrined in the civil societies of Greece and Rome. So, David, the original ideal was praiseworthy."

"Then what happened?" David asked Angelica.

Angelica answered, "Unfortunately, we know from history that power corrupts and absolute power corrupts absolutely. So this is what happened: when the

Illuminati revived themselves in the 1700s, they were able to do so because the dark negative energy present in the cosmos managed to find its way to Earth and spawned the Illuminati. The seed of corrupt power and control took root and took over power in: (1) The international giant companies—they are well organized and control the pricing of all the goods and services, (2) the giant financial institutions, insurance companies and pharmaceutical giants which control the flow of money, and (3) the arms dealers whose very livelihood depends on warring factions. These three make up the 7,000000 of the people in control of the Earth and most of the Billionaires, otherwise known as the Illuminati—now there is an oxymoron."

Responding to the conversation, SuperBeing Sara spoke up saying. "We must take control of all the telecommunications systems which are used for military purposes globally. This is easily accomplished."

Next the third SuperBeing, Teresa, said "Once we have control over all the telecommunication systems we can address all Spiritual Beings (People) on planet Earth. They will see all of us and hear only the one Pleiades Representative from their area. I believe we can neutralize all their means of waging war—both mechanical and computerized."

SuperBeing Teresa continued, "You see, David, we have the awesome power to manipulate matter. People on Earth manipulate matter as well, but the difference is that your people manipulate matter by the use of chemical, metallurgical and mechanical knowledge. For example, to make a car you use oil to make plastics, iron and other metals to make steel and sand to make glass. It is magic in a crude way; however, to us it is obsolete as this type of magic takes a lot of time and labor."

David listened intently, but what SuperBeing Teresa told him next really blew his mind.

SuperBeing Teresa said, "A hundred thousand years ago we learned the very nature of who we are: Spiritual Light Beings. We manipulate matter through the power of our thoughts. We transform matter only in a genre of constructive loving use of Creation's Energy."

"How do you do that?" David asked.

"You see, David, we are the Light. So you will understand better, here is an example of what happens when we use our Light Energy. We shoot a beam of light which contains two things: (1) a QL (Quantum Love) Gene—this gene is a Light Loving Energy gene which easily removes the dark negative destructive Energy, and (2) a teleportation energizer that is enclosed in a beam of Light. The result is that when one of our Light beams hits the Bad Guy he is not killed, but instead instantly transformed into a Good Guy. This *transformed* Good Guy now is endowed with Light Energy."

"Wow!" David said, "It's hard to believe that you can really change Bad Guys into Good Guys. It sounds like very advanced magic to me ... like right out of a Sci-Fi story."

SuperBeing Teresa smiled and said, "I should

make something very clear. This is for real and actually quite scientific. You see, David, energy is neutral and very real. For example, it can be used to cook your meal or cook the man. Love is very real. It is the positive use of Energy. Once the Quantum Love Gene has completed its work, the teleportation energizer that is encoded within the Quantum Love Gene teleports the Bad Guy that is now transformed into a Good Guy back to his home world. Pretty cool, hey?"

David just sat there with a numb smile. Then as if suddenly awakened, he burst out, "Wow, that's fantastic. We could sure use that teleportation energizer here!"

Sharia chirped in saying, "I think we need to consolidate our strength by working with the metaphysical community. There is even one metaphysical organization of influential 'Some-bodies' whose mantra is: *Awakening Humanity to its Spiritual Magnificence.*"

Sara said, "We need to unite with an enlightened spiritual group because as we execute our plans, David envisions a possible strong negative reaction from the entire religious community with a lesser negative reaction from the Eastern philosophies."

Dream #20, March 20, 2009
Contact

… as related by Angelica to David

John Elsworth, the senior astronomer at the SETTI station was a solitary man of about 45. He was a professor at MIT, head of the Astronomy department until his dear wife, whom he loved very much, passed away from breast cancer. Cecilia was forty and John was forty-two. Their two children, named Andre and Sherri, were married. John was devastated. He took a leave of absence from MIT, but being alone without Cecilia was too much. He stumbled across a job as Senior Astronomer at the famous SETTI observatory. He took the job realizing that he would not have much contact with people. This seemed like a good choice because all he wanted was to be left alone.

0700 hours:

John was suddenly awakened from his usual unscheduled nap by a very distinct alarm from his computer. It was the alarm he was hoping to hear someday in his lifetime, the one that signaled the presence of intelligent movement of objects or Beings thousands of light years away.

As the alarm sounded it took John a few minutes to readjust to—to get hold of—the present moment. This was an extremely unlikely event to happen, and yet it had just happened.

In response to the alarm, John jumped off the couch and leaped forward onto his rolling chair. He stared at the monitor for confirmation. Sure enough the monitor, which usually showed a specific star pattern, was now lit up with thousands of little red dots flashing at him. John quickly rechecked the authenticity of what he is witnessing. After the fourth check he stopped and simply stared at the dots. The data was telling John that since he started looking at this event the objects had travelled more than ten light years—all in about two minutes.

John realized that he had a certain protocol to follow. He must call his boss in New York.

David looked at Angelica and said, "Angelica, how do you know all this inside stuff?

Angelica answered, "We have been monitoring Earth for a long time."

About ready to make the call, John heard the phone already ringing—the *red* one, the *Emergency Direct Line* to the President.

"Oh, my God!" John thought, "I'm going to talk to the President of the USA." Meanwhile John kept his eyes riveted on the monitor.

John picked up the old-style, chorded, red phone and managed to say, "Hello, this is Dr. John Elsworth."

At the other end of the line John heard a very disturbed but controlled voice, "This is President Castrorez. Dr. Elsworth, are you looking at your monitor?"

John answered, "Yes, I am looking at it, Mr. President."

"Can you tell me what you see?" President Castrorez asked.

"Yes, Mr. President," John replied, "I see thousands, actually ten thousand and one objects rapidly approaching Earth. They will be in Earth's orbit in about thirty seconds, Sir."

Mr. President asked, "Can you determine any other information such as size, configuration, etc.?"

John answered, "Yes, Mr. President, but your military satellites and radar can do a much better job now that they are in orbit. At about 2,000 km from Earth … "

Click, the red phone went dead.

Each morning I wake up anticipating the new dream. What will I write about today? 10,000 ships in orbit … wow!

Dream #21, March 21, 2009
10,000 Ships in Orbit:
Friends or Enemies?

0735 hours

Angelica said to David, "Now the fun begins. Our 10,001 ships have arrived in orbit around Earth."

Suddenly all of Earth's defense systems were on high red alert, only it wasn't an Earthly threat ... that is, not from one country to another. The threat was a very strange appearance in the sky as seen on long range telescopes. Thousands of objects were observed approaching Earth. According to NASA, these objects seemed to be uniformly spaced and moving at incredible speeds with very specific trajectories. This indicated a deliberate target—Earth!

Angelica, telepathically watching the action, interjected a comment, "It is interesting to note that Earth people assume instantly that whatever is coming must be a threat."

Suddenly John's astronomical wizards/telescopes became useless.

Two minutes and thirty seconds after the alarm went off at the Setti Astronomical station, General Stafford, head of the NATO Allies said to the US President, just as he disconnected from his call with

John, "Mr. President, we are surrounded by 10,000 very large ships in Earth's orbit at about 2,000 km. They appear like bright stars to our naked eye. We have confirmed their presence on radar."

The President of NATO, Mr. Wilson, made a brief call to President Hu Lintao of China. He said, "Mr. President, greetings. First, I'm sure we can agree that what is in Earth's orbit at 2,000 km is not of a World Power's doing, right?"

"Yes, Mr. Wilson," President Hu Lintao assured him, "on this we can agree. But you understand that for domestic political reasons I have placed our defense system on full ready alert."

"I understand," Mr. Wilson replied. He then continued, "Would you agree we should place our Earth's defense systems on Red Full High Alert at the same time we simultaneously engage in a global video conference call with all major countries? You do agree, don't you, that we need to do everything possible to avoid a global conflict?"

"Yes," replied President Lintao, "I definitely agree. It's obvious we are facing a much greater threat to Earth than from each other. Reports from all over the world are coming in to news organizations of strange sightings by astronomers and amateur observers. The reports range from observations of UFOs to stars and meteorites. What seems to be clear is the sheer numbers. Some reports say that the skies are completely disoriented as thousands of new stars light up the sky from every part of the planet. Some observers with telescopes report they see weird shapes like snails.

They believe these shapes are very large judging from their distance from us. Yes, all this is happening right now."

Privy to their conversation, President Dr. Yu Lang of the UN decided to make an announcement. Dr. Yu Lang addressed all members of the Security Council via video conferencing, "Because there simply is not enough time to meet at the UN, I am talking to you via video conferencing. Ladies and Gentlemen and all representatives of member states of this UN, we have an emergency. We are facing what seems like a cosmic intervention of human affairs. As you all know, Earth is surrounded by approximately 10,000 very large objects, probably ships. They are in Earth's orbit at about 2,000 km. Although we do not have any communication from these intruders yet, nor have we experienced any hostile action ... wait, I'm getting a message from DNN TV from a reporter, Ann Adams, special attaché to the UN."

Dr. Yu Wong Lee started conversing with Miss Adams, "Miss Adams, this is President of the UN Security council, Dr. Yu Lang. Do you have a report?"

"Yes," replied Miss Adams. "Sir, I have just been informed that all telecommunications on Earth are about to be ... ."

I reluctantly put my pen down. I think, "Angelica sure knows how to create suspense. I'm sure I will hear about it tomorrow."

Dream #22, March 22, 2009
Direct Contact

Before she could finish, Miss Adam's call was interrupted by a stranger's voice coming over the speakers. The voice said, "My name is Angelica. Please do not panic. We come in peace. It is extremely important that I speak to the people of Earth. Mr. President of the UN, Dr. Yu Lee, I apologize for this breach of diplomacy."

President Yu Lee responded with a question, "Are your intentions hostile or peaceful? Where are you calling from? Where are you?"

Angelica replied, "We are representatives of the Galactic Federation of Planets. I assure you that our intentions are entirely peaceful, as a matter of fact, we have been invited by several of your people to assist in the pending solar alignment with the center of our galaxy and the inevitable arrival of the massive Black Hole. I speak to you from our mother ship called Starship Cosmos. Starship Cosmos is in orbit—2,000 km from Earth above San Fransisco."

President Yu Lee responded, "Given that you have already breached all our security protocols and no doubt have the capacity to address the world without my permission, you are being very diplomatic. So, yes, please continue and state your purpose. But wait! Please understand that we the people of earth are prepared to defend ourselves."

Angelica replied, "Thank you Mr. President. I now

speak to all nations on Earth. I speak to you all your languages and dialects. I also address your Special UN Security Council. First, let me be absolutely clear. We are no threat to you. We only have peaceful, loving intentions. We come because many of you have invited us, and because you are our descendants. *You are our descendants!* We are Pleiadians from the Pleiades star system near the Taurus cluster. Your Greek ancestors named us Pleiades, also known by more recent historians as the Seven Sisters. It is our intention to help Earth people survive your inevitable encounter with an approaching Black Hole. So that we can help you, we have been monitoring all your telecommunication systems."

The voice of Angelica faded away and Dr. Yu Lee of the UN Security Council continued, "Now, let's simply pause for a moment. Okay, here we are: Six billion people pretty much split on the subject of aliens, and Boom! Here we are listening to what sounds like an ordinary female voice, but, the woman claims she is from Pleiades, therefore, she is an alien and is being heard all over the world. Things are beginning to get really weird."

Angelica heard Dr. Yu Lee and responded, "Okay, I know all this is pretty weird and frightening. Look! Please get this straight. We are the Good Guys and you are our descendants. We come to offer our assistance. Earth is about to go through a massive shredder, the Black Hole; however, we have the technology with 10,000 ships to render this Black Hole harmless. Now, despite our incredible capabilities, we cannot help unless a majority of Earth people decide to make a shift. By making a shift, I mean to make the leap from a *fear*-based philosophy to a *love*-based reality. This evolutionary jump is absolutely necessary to safely pass through the Black Hole approaching the center of our Galaxy … more about this later."

0743 hours

After pausing to let her audience catch their breaths, Angelica informed them of what she and the other Pleiades helpers were doing, "Now to make things go as easily as possible we are *as of now* taking complete control of all of Earth's telecommunication's technology. All TV broadcasts are *as of this moment* cancelled and every channel in every language is cancelled. From this moment forward, all you will hear and see will be through and by our system. As soon as this catastrophe has passed and Earth's climate is re-established, all TV and radio stations will be restored back to order. Then we will leave as quickly as we came."

All military hardware and software, all arms of any kind are as of this moment nullified—rendered harmless material. This is in effect in all countries all over the world."

Please do not be alarmed. We mean you *no harm*. Right now as I speak, our mother ship should be visible to you as we are only 200 km from Earth. From here we will "beam down" I think that is the right term according to your entertainment you call Sci-Fi movies. Five of our people have already beamed down and are meeting with your Earthling named David Chartrand. Although we Pleiadians primarily exist in non-corporeal state in the fifth dimension (we don't have to inhabit a body), we can easily shift into your three-dimensional reality with body. This will make your adjustment to our presence easier."

My, this is turning out to be an interesting story ... scary and exciting. This time I find myself in a big room onboard the Pleiadian mother ship, Starship Cosmos.

Dream #23, March 23, 2009
Onboard the Pleiadian
Mother Ship, Starship Cosmos

And so it began. All telecommunications over the entire world were jammed and in the control of the Pleiadians. All military capabilities were neutralized, that is, all Nukes, all shells, all arms factories, all Nuke subs, all military aircraft and military computer systems … all of it, all over the planet simultaneously went down at 0743 hours. Apparently the Pleiadians have the ability to transform matter into anything they desire with their minds.

Pleiadian Being Sara had been listening to a number of arms dealers. She listened in to and recorded the conversation of retired Secretary of Defense, Mr. Armstrong then broadcasted it out over TV for the whole world to hear. Mr. Armstrong was saying, "We have the means and the power to crush those outside Do-gooders. What right do they have in meddling with human affairs? We have a right and responsibility to sell arms to whomever we choose as long as they support American interests."

Sara overrode Mr. Armstrong and spoke to the TV listening audience. "Oh! By the way, Mr. Armstrong is recognized by the Bushnell family, the largest arms dealer."

Sara then switched back to Mr. Armstrong. Mr. Armstrong was interrupted by one of his men saying,

"Mr. Armstrong, Sir, our entire computer network just went off line. We don't know who the perpetrator is. Wait, here it comes on again. But wait! What the hell is this? Who are these multi colored women and what the hell is going on? And look—that egotistical Canadian big shot David character is with them."

Fred, Junior Officer in charge of communications announced, "Chief Armstrong, it looks like they have complete telecommunication control ... world-wide. Sir, it looks like one of them is talking in English and on TV."

Chief Armstrong replied, "Well, turn it up. We may as well listen. Maybe we can find a weakness, a crack in their armor."

They turned up the volume and this is what they heard, "My name is Angelica. Please do not be alarmed. We have temporary control over all of Earth's Telecommunications. *The only* purpose of this is to facilitate communication all over the world. We are not a threat. Our presence is peaceful. Our purpose here is to help you pass through the Black Hole rapidly approaching Earth. As most of you know, *all* inhabitants of Earth are presently in danger due to Earth's coming alignment with the center of our Galaxy and the approaching Black Hole ... not to mention your path of self-destruction."

This was a short dream, but very profound. I think "Is this really about to happen?"

Dream #24, March 24, 2009
Deal or No Deal

Angelica explained the conditions to Earth's people. "Please be aware that if you vote No to our offer we will honor that decision of 'No Deal,' and we will leave as quickly as we came. If you vote to accept our offer to help, then as part of our deal, Earth will be saved. This is what will happen."

First, using the awesome power of each of our ships, we will form a protective shield around Earth which will allow Earth to pass through the deadly Black Hole unharmed."

We will re-terra form Earth to a previous level of 2,000 years ago."

We will help you develop a socio-economic model which will benefit all of your ethnic groups and countries. As a result of your evolutionary jump, greed, competition, the accumulation of unlimited wealth will be replaced with cooperation and an unprecedented growth in individual creativity. Space travel will become common place."

We will provide you with the knowledge of how to use the awesome energy of this planet to fuel all your homes, cars and other transportation. The use of fossil/carbon-based fuels will be obsolete."

It is imperative that you understand that in order to evolve to the fifth dimension you need to accept and embrace who you truly are. You are an individualized Spirit Light Being. You are non corporeal, and you choose to be in a human body. Your ancestors are Pleiadian."

We humbly ask you when it comes time for you to vote on our proposal that you think with your heart."

After Angelica stopped speaking there was dead silence over the airways. The whole world was so silent you could hear a pin drop.

Dream #25, March 25, 2009
Sara and her Telepathic Powers

Breaking the silence, Sara spoke, "I am telepathic in both sound and sight. I can and am listening to whomever I want to anywhere on your planet. Please understand that it is not our intention to snoop in anyone's private life. We are only interested in intelligence that has to do with the activity of the Illuminati. No lead or other substance can hinder my telepathic ability. I will rebroadcast sound and image through your televisions with live conversations taking place; for example, right now in Washington, DC, a member of the Joint Chiefs of Staff, John Candu and Victor Boutter, the biggest arms dealer in the world, are engaged in a conversation. Here is the broadcast on channel 03"

John Candu was speaking "... and I'm telling you this in absolute confidence. We will not allow the destruction of our missiles, planes, etc. We need the ability to defend—no, we need the ability to strike first with all the power we can muster. We need that secret non-gravity EMP (Electro-magnetic-pulse) bomber. Hell, its stealth, right? Yes, that's right, and it makes a non-signature sound. But wait, you have not heard the best news yet."

John then paused for a moment.

Victor looked at John with a look of "well ... this is supposed to be America's top Secret of all time ... I mean, we are talking about *the* secret!"

John said, "Victor, Victor, can you hear me?"

Victor snapped out of it. He replied to John in a sheepish half smile and sinister killer instinct look, "John do you have any idea what this bird can do?"

"No!" John responded, "tell me."

Victor hesitated, wringing his hands and clearly agitated knowing he was about to let loose the biggest, maddest, meanest weapon of all time.

John sensed his hesitation and grabbed Victor's arm, looked him in the eyes and said in a very commanding voice, "We need your EMP aircraft, your EMF guns. Together we need to destroy this alien threat and blame it on China before it destroys us. Hell, they will pin the highest medal on us and we will be heroes for saving the Earth from an alien invasion."

Sweat now pouring off of his face, Victor stared at the TV in disbelief and replied, "I don't believe what I'm hearing and seeing on the TV."

John spun around in stunned comprehension and said to Victor, "I'll be damned. It looks like we are seeing the same thing on our TVs. I see you and me talking and this private conversation has just been heard by the whole world." John slammed his fist against the table yelling at the top of his voice, "Is someone in Hollywood producing this crap?"

In desperation, John looked around the room wondering where the camera was and who was producing the videos. Feeling extremely vulnerable and powerless, John screamed, "Turn the damn TV off. At least I won't have to see myself on TV. I hear the

President believes it—damn bleeding heart liberal Democrat. What are we going to do about this? We better get on this right away. It's going to be hard. All our communications are out."

John said, "Okay, so the whole world heard that including the US President. It is not a Hollywood production. You see these real, known people live on your TV all over the world."

Good and Evil, Final Battle

Good and Evil forces have been at war for more than five hundred thousand years. The evil forces are those which are identified as using the energy (God, the universe) in a destructive negative way. The good forces are those which are identified as using energy in a positive loving expanding way. The evil force is the Lucifarian Empire ruled by the master destroyer and master of the dark use of Energy King Lucifer. He rules from the planet Diable on the far side of the Milky Way Galaxy. It is said in legends that Lucifer was a master of masters of the Light, good use of Energy, and that he was persuaded to the dark side by the very powerful War Lord Dementor from another Galaxy far away with the intoxicating promise of becoming ruler of his own Empire. And thus he became the ruthless king of the Lucifarian Empire. It stretches more than 50,000 parsecs across and covers close to 5,000 humanoid worlds. King Lucifer is possessed with his thirst for power and thus to conquer The Intergalactic Federation of Planets. That may seem big, but the good guys known as the Intergalactic Federation of Planets (IFOP) spreads across 100 Galaxies and 50,000 humanoid planets. The number of Solar systems is not known but closest estimate is 10,000,000,000.

Things have been going well for the IFOP in the Milky Way galaxy as the Pleiadian-led assault by Fleet Commander Ulanda has resulted in the conversion of many Lucifarian Systems. This is primarily due to their new secret weapon which will be described shortly.

The Final Assault

Deep in space the war between the Dark Force, The Lucifarian Empire and the Light Force, The Intergalactic Federation of Planets, rages on. However, this war in the Milky Way galaxy seems to be drawing down. The Lucifarian Empire is led by a ruthless half man half machine General by the name of Duke Vandor. He is a master of the dark use of energy and Supreme Commander of all Lucifarian forces. Vandor lives and breathes to conquer all living planets of the Milky Way in the name of his ruler and master Lucifer.

Duke Vandor arrived at Planet Diable where he met with King Lucifer. As the Duke knelt before his King he said, "Your Majesty, Vandor is at your humble service."

"My trusted warrior stand," said King Lucifer. Looking the Duke straight in the eyes, he leaned over a little and said with a stern angry voice, "You are the leader of all my armies, why have we not conquered the IFOP?"

Duke Vandor dropped to his knees fearing the powerful king's wrath. "My men were returning from the front lines as though they were teleported back. But worse than that, your majesty, they seemed to be transformed somehow into peaceful men without a word of explanation. My best interrogators have used every technique we know, and we simply cannot find a single shred of evidence or reason why they have returned in this manner. We have interrogated at least 1,000 of them, and unfortunately I have to report that they didn't make it. They died under investigation and torture without us gaining a single piece of information.

At this point, the Duke chanced a glance at the King. He raised his head to dare a look into his eyes and feel the wrath. He was right to fear the King's wrath as the King raised his hand, pointed it at the Duke and lightning bolts struck the Duke with such force as to knock him back onto the floor. This continued for about ten seconds.

Then the king sat down and said to his Duke, "You may get up. You know very well, Duke Vandor, failure is not acceptable. Yet you come to me with this story, this tale of the thousand men, because you can't get correct information from them about why they have come back like a bunch of sheep. Nonetheless, my faith is not totally lost in you. You have one more chance to redeem yourself. I want you to lead the attack force against the Pleiadians who are now surrounding the planet Earth with 10,000 ships supposedly to save them from their pending peril with the Black Hole. Take as many ships and men as you can from all the systems from here to Earth. If you fail, do not come back. Do you understand?

Duke Vandor still on his knees, still trembling from the incredible electrical shocks he had just received from his King, dared to speak, "Thank you, my Lord, I will do as you ask and I will not fail lest my life be forfeited as you have commanded your majesty."

The King waved his hand as if to say, get out of here, get out of my sight. Duke Vandor then slowly rose from his knees and still in pain from the shocks and not daring to look at his master, slowly turned around and skulked away. Once out of the king's chambers Duke Vandor slammed his fist against the wall and swore beneath his breath, "I will kill every single one of those sheep-like returnees until I find the truth about this impossible event. This secret weapon of the Pleiadians must be disclosed to my people if we are to defeat them." As he left the palace, the Duke turned to his first Lieut. and said, "Gather all these so-called sheep, these peaceful men, and bring to me the best of the best interrogators you have. We must find out this secret weapon that brings my soldiers back to this planet, like sheep. Go."

Vandor went from planet to planet gathering and interrogating every single returnee from the battle that mysteriously arrived as a good guy. Ten of his best investigators went to work with every technique and ability. They had to find out what indeed had happened and yet the mystery remained. Duke Vandor was very careful to advise his top soldiers to never reveal this truth to his King, or he would execute them himself.

In the meantime, Duke Vandor gathered his

armies and 20,000 ships and headed for Earth. He was determined to conquer the Intergalactic Federation of Planets and redeem himself to His Majesty King Lucifer.

At that time the Lucifarian Empire was ruler of 25% of all living planets in the Milky Way Galaxy. However in the past 10,000 years Lucifer's Dark Energy grip had been slipping rapidly. The cause of this slip seems to be from his own realm. It bears repeating that many of his trusted soldiers suddenly appeared among his people. Soldiers who were last accounted for as being in the front lines of the battles against the Enemy, the Intergalactic Federation of Planets. But wait a minute, these soldiers returning seemed very different than they did going into battle. Besides what in the name of Lucifer were they doing here? They were the best of the best fighters of the Lucifarian Empire. Oh my! Trouble in the Empire.

0637 hours to Alignment, Omega, The End

The Dark Force under the command of Duke Vandor attempted to take the battle to Earth to assist the dark energy of the Illuminati deep underground locked in their very plush hideout. It seemed that 100 one-man attack aircraft had broken formation, scattered to disrupt the very powerful IFOP Force which had destroyed 85% of their 20,000 battle ships. The Lucifarian attackers planned to rendezvous about 200 kilometers above the dark side of Mars. There, they planned to go to warp speed and reappear in a 20,000 kilometer orbit of Earth and proceed with a surprise attack on the 10,000 Pleiades star ships orbiting Earth at 2,000 kilometers. They were specifically targeting Starship Cosmos where the Pleiades and Earth representatives were meeting.

Vandor said to his number one, "Go to warp on my mark 3, 2, 1 … mark." One hundred ships jumped to warp drive. In two minutes they reached their objective of a 2,000 kilometer orbit above Earth.

030201 hours to Alignment, Omega, End

One hundred Lucifarian attack fighters have jumped out of warp and appeared in a 2,000 km orbit around Earth.

The Pleiadians, under the command of Cmdr. Yolanda, were caught off guard, since they did not detect the new Lucifarian Army hiding behind Mars. However, Cmdr. Yolanda dispatched 10 of her top ships to attack the incoming 100 enemy attack vessels. It is very difficult to engage the enemy while in warp drive. Yolanda's ships were gaining on the Lucifarian ships rapidly at 100 times the speed of light. The Lucifarian battle cruisers have a mere speed of 10 times the speed of light.

Let us now turn to the meeting on Starship Cosmos which is about to take place.

024249 hours to Alignment, Omega, the End

Dream #25, March 25

About 10 minutes into the meeting, loud explosions were heard in rapid succession. A bright light show appeared in the skies far above Earth like a fireworks show, but it was like stars lighting up and disappearing. The show was from the warp drive of the Lucifarian Attack Fighters as they shifted from warp drive to EM Pulse drive. (When a ship breaks from warp to sublite speed, a bright light flash is emitted much like a sonic boom with sound blasts of 750 mph.)

The Pleiadian military, in Earth's orbit under the command of General Willway received the communication from their sister ships in battle just one minute before the Lucifarian ships were to break warp and appear 2,000 kilometers before them in a surprise attack. Ten Pleiadian, one-person attack fighters called *Darts* from the 10,000 stationed around Earth went to *red alert* battle mode. They were able to target 97of the 100 Darthanian Attack Fighters a nanosecond after they went from warp drive to EMPulse drive.

0109 hours to Alignment, Omega, the End

The Pleiadians are masters at the art of altering matter, they *do not kill the enemy*. They employ the positive use of energy. It's the same as Universal Energy, or Divine Intelligence or God. They have been trained for 100,000 years in the art of transmuting matter into whatever they want by choosing to focus positive Loving thoughts. This is loving use of energy. General Willway ordered 5,000 of her most advanced transmitters aboard the 10,000 ships in Earth's orbit to target the incoming attackers and all their torpedoes, infiltrate their technology and alter the 3 dimensional matter of the Lucifarian Armament from weapons of mass destruction to harmless material objects. This was accomplished in nano seconds. It is important to note that each of these Lucifarian small attackers were a one-person craft and that none of the people were killed. Rather they were infiltrated by a very powerful QLGene Beam. These beams contain a Quantum Love Gene (QLG) and a teleportation transponder programmed to send the pilot back to the Lucifarian home world. Can you imagine the looks on their faces when they suddenly found themselves back on their home planet smack in the middle of dark angry negative family members and fellow soldiers?

002934 hours to Alignment, Omega, The End

Three of these small attackers got through, but not for long; however, they managed to target three of the Pleiadian ships with five photon torpedoes aimed at each of them. The Pleiadians, using their QLGene Beam transmuted these three attackers. All but one torpedo was transmuted by the QLGene Beam long before it reached its targets. The remaining torpedo approaching the Pleiades' Starship Cosmo was transmuted also by the QLGene Beam —not from its own ship, but from three Sisters flying at 100 km/sec. Using their QLGene Beam they transmuted these remaining 10 torpedoes into harmless Energy. The attack was over and had failed completely. No harm had come to Earth or to the Pleiadians.

David addressed the delegates, "Just a few moments ago, a last desperate attempt by Lucifer and his Dark Energy Beings attacked our star ships surrounding Earth. They even attacked this ship with 10 photon torpedoes while we were in session. The torpedoes were all transmuted by 30 of our warriors, all of their pilots were transmuted to positive Energy and teleported back to their home planet."

The battle in space was over.

Angelica tells me at the beginning of Dream #26, "Raymond, I am going to go back **to Sand**y, David and Myra the dolphin."

Dream #26, March 26, 2009
Sandy and Myra Meet Again.
David has a Big Surprise from Myra.

Dr. Sandy Travers, the director of Citation research at the UC Marine Laboratory, was an activist involved in protests against the "one percent, the Illuminati, the bad guys." Sandy went unnoticed into the control room which oversees the Dolphin pools. Her intuition told her to communicate with Myra in an effort to understand what happened the other day when she spoke to Myra about a Black Hole image. The overwhelming pain in her head needed to be explained and resolved. Sandy decided to talk to Myra directly. She approached the dolphin pool and posed her question to Myra, "Is there a danger, is the big black something a nothing, and is it a doorway? Myra … a doorway? Is the back door the Black Hole?" Myra leapt into the air with excitement while chattering. Her answer was obviously affirmative and it was translated both vocally and telepathically, "Yes, yes, the Black Hole is approaching and is yet to be experienced."

Myra then went on to explain to Sandy that the sudden pain Sandy was experiencing was because she, Myra, has miscalculated Sandy's capacity to process a very large burst of negative imagery of the Black Hole. Myra apologized to Sandy.

Sandy had befriended David Chartrand at a conference on universal translation where David unveiled his new Universal Translator. Sandy had asked David if he could invent software to include the dolphins in his Universal Translator. David assured Sandy that he would do just that and would do it easily, A.S.A.P.

Sandy touched a metal round object in her pocket. She pulled it out and realized with joy that it was a telecommunication devise David had given her. Sandy flipped open the communicator pushed the talk button and said, "David, this is Sandy can you hear me.

A moment later David replied, "Yes Sandy I can hear you and it's so good to hear your voice."

Sandy said, "David, would you like to meet at the coffee shop across the street? I mean can you beam down?"

"Yes absolutely, I will use the communicator as the coordinates, make sure you are clear of objects or people OK?

Sandy said, "OK I am clear." Three seconds later David appeared facing Sandy.

They sat down in a booth at the coffee shop. Sandy said, "Remember the black-out experience you had at the Dolphin pool?"

David replied, "Yes, how could I forget? That was pretty freaky."

Sandy continued "I want you to come back to the pool. I think I can help you with that. Also David, remember that injection you got from Dr. Reinhart? Ever since then you seem to have blocked out memories of your mother. David, take a look at this drawing."

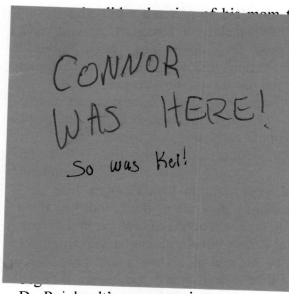

ward David.
ck of pain.
elepathically
einhardt."
pain and yet
Emotionally

o the Marine
se repressed

ft the coffee
Lab to meet
the pool the
and blasting
visions David
mother broke
Dr. Reinhardt's programming.

Next David focused on Myra and jumped into the pool to greet her. David placed a necklace around Myra's neck. The pendant was David's latest invention, the new universal translator including the Dolphin language. Myra gently rubbed her big dolphin nose against David's chest. Then Myra looked up at David with her big crystal brown eyes and telepathically and audibly said, "David I have something to give you that my species has been holding for 10,000 years."

Via the Universal Translator, everything Myra said was heard in English and seen by everyone throughout the planet on TV. Of course, this was received with a loud applause.

Myra said to David, "Please put the palms of your hands on each side of my temple." David complied joyfully. Myra then said, repeat after me, "I, David, accept and embody this Quantum Love Gene."

David repeated Myra's words.

Myra continued, "I know I am a Spirit-Light Being incarnated in this human form." Again David repeated her words. Myra said, "I now release and transfer the Golden Key to the three Quantum Love Genes to you, David Chartrand."

One small very bright golden ball of light was seen leaving Myra's temple. It danced around David's head for a full five seconds before disappearing into David's temple.

Responding to the transfer of light, David gave Myra a big hug. Silence ensued … not a sound for at least five seconds. David suddenly felt a surge of gentle electric shock-like waves move through his entire body down to the very depth of his DNA. Inner space and outer space seemed to coalesce. An incredible power of love swept through David.

David released Myra, looked into her loving eyes and whispered, "Thank you, thank you for believing in us and holding our Quantum Love Gene for 10,000 years."

Myra laughed shaking her head up and down. "David" she said, "always remember that you have not one but three Quantum Love Genes!"

David was stunned but before he could react, Myra invited David to play with her. He accepted and grabbed hold of Myra's dorsal fin. Myra swam wildly about the pool taking David on the fastest and most thrilling ride of his life. Thirty seconds later, David was totally exhausted as Myra slowed down and came to rest at the side of the pool.

As David let go of Myra's dorsal fin, he turned around and made eye contact with Myra's big beautiful brown eyes. David said to her, "Myra, I thank you. Thank you for this amazing, incredible gift. The fact that your species has kept this Quantum Love Gene generation after generation for 10,000 years is in itself an astounding achievement. Obviously you too embody this Quantum Love Gene. You see, Myra, when I think about dolphins I think of all the love, grace and astonishing beauty that you are and behold."

Expressing his gratitude, David extended his arm and put it around Myra's neck giving Myra his farewell oath, "Myra I will repeat this ceremony of the Quantum Love Gene transfer to all of the people of Earth"

Myra nudged up against David and said loud enough that everyone present could hear her, "Together we will take the next big jump in evolution. This awakening will spread across the globe many times faster than anyone could imagine." Then Myra swam even closer to David and whispered in his ear, "David, perhaps Sandy could be your first initiation?"

David climbed out of the pool. Turning to Sandy, he looked her in the eyes, smiled and said, "Sandy do you wish to receive this Quantum Love Gene?"

Sandy looked at David with nothing but love in her eyes. For a second David was distracted by the forceful power of Sandy's love, then he recovered and said, "Okay, Sandy, please place the palms of your hands on my temples. Wait! Now is the time for all of my Pleiadian brothers and sisters on Earth to repeat what I say. If there's someone close to you put your hands on their temples and prepare to receive the key to your Quantum Love Gene buried deep in your consciousness."

Sandy slowly and deliberately placed the palms of her hands on David's temple—all the time maintaining eye contact with David.

David said, "Repeat after me. I, Sandy Travers, accept and embody this Quantum Love Gene."

Sandy repeated, "I, Sandy Travers, accept and embody this Quantum Love Gene."

Then David asked Sandy to also repeat after him, "I am Spirit Light Being incarnated in human form."

Sandy repeated his words, "I am Spirit Light Being incarnated in human form."

David then said, "I pass on to you the Golden Key to the Quantum Love Gene."

Sandy replied, "I, Sandy, receive this Key to the Quantum Love Gene."

There was silence for about five seconds. Then, in the midst of the silence a small golden bright ball of light left David's temple. The ball of light danced around Sandy's head and then disappeared into Sandy's temple.

Sandy let go of David's temples. She wrapped her arms around David and they embraced. Encircling them was a visible glow of golden light, a glow of Love

120

Dream #26, March 26

Energy.

David finally released Sandy, but not before giving her a slow deliberate loving kiss. David turned to the camera and said to the world, "The kiss part is optional!"

What happened next was nothing less than a miracle. All of the representatives in this momentous time joined in and began to repeat Myra's ceremony. This of course was seen by anyone on Earth with a TV.

Myra jumped out of the water smiling and saying, "Whoopee!" Myra continued her wild jumping up and down as she yelled, "Love is all around us!"

Meanwhile Sandy was experiencing her own transformation as jolts of energy surged through her. She felt a sudden overwhelming sense of joy, love and power. She looked around making deliberate eye contact with everyone and proclaimed, "I am Spirit Being! I love all of you!" Sandy declared, "Let's do this, let's transform this world into what it was 2,000 years ago.

Myra was quick to point out that from now on everyone who participates in the ceremony will experience the Quantum Love Gene from *within* glowing and awakening their own genetic helix.

I can't wait to continue the dream. The plot is thickening. Angelica can sure tell a good story. I'm now totally captivated. Can't wait to pick up my pen and listen to the dream. It's a little frustrating because sometimes I can't seem to write fast enough for the thoughts that come through. It's uncanny because it seems like the story is almost dictated to me ... like I'm writing down, word for word, from the dream. It's simply weird.

Dream #27, March 27, 2009
Angelica's Message

Pleiadian Spokesperson Angelica spoke from her Starship Cosmos, "My name is Angelica. I now wish to address all Beings on this home we call Earth. What you have heard and seen is in Real Time. Conversations are being heard all over the developed world. Every conversation can be broadcast globally in any language. There is total transparency. We do this *not* to intimidate or control you. We are simply using your technology and our technology to communicate with you and reassure you of your safety. We can hear and see the Bad Guys in action whenever we choose."

Please bear with me. I'm going to repeat myself because it's very important that you understand. We are not interested in personal conversations of love, peace and people's everyday lives. We don't peep into people's bedrooms nor do we invade anyone's private lives. We are, however, most interested in exposing the negative dark energy of the planet controlled by the Illuminati, the one percent, the elite rich and the super-powerful. So, to everyone using negative, dark energy: Be forewarned! The whole world *knows* what you are up to."

Angelica continued to talk to Earth's people in an effort to dispel fear by creating understanding. She explained, "Ten thousand years ago we Pleiadians had forgotten who and what we are, i.e., *non-physical* Spiritual Light Beings. This forgetfulness happened

123

even though the second wave of Pleiadians had been on Earth twelve thousand years. The once paradise of light and love energy on Earth was overwhelmed by the dark negative forces of fear, greed and power. So we lost our way and *survival of the fittest* took over on Earth. Power and wealth became the ultimate goals. Striving to attain these goals was fueled by the abuse of religions and put into action by the Illuminati. The weapon of success called Divide and Conquer was born. Cooperation was replaced with competition. War was used as a legitimate way of attainment. Fear was born and soon became the cause and creation of the greatest myth ever: that there exists *an enemy!* And so here we are in the twenty-first century still oppressed by Dark Energy. There are false perceptions of something called 'enemies' which perpetuates a cycle of war and peace. Spanning thousands of years there has been control of many by a few. Much to the surprise of many people, evidence of this has become fact according to research done by the UN."

Angelica then rallied her audience as she said, "Earth people, AWAKEN! It is time to join this global transformation! As we have said, *all* of you who choose to awaken will shift to the next time line, the fifth dimension. You will become the embodiment of the true nature of *Who* and *What* you are: a *spiritual non-corporeal Light Being!* At the moment of Alignment, your QL (Quantum Love) Gene will be activated. It has been asleep for ten thousand years. We have only one goal, and that is to provide you with an opportunity to shift your consciousness from the third dimension of

124

physical reality to the fifth dimension. It is this shift that will save you and the planet from certain environmental destruction.

Again I cannot overemphasize the fact that this decision is yours, not ours. Once your planet and all its Beings have passed through the Black Hole, we will disappear as quickly as we appeared. We can do this because we travel by intention, by thoughts. This is *the* deciding moment!"

Dream #28, March 28, 2009
Our Record as Custodians of this Beautiful Planet

At this point David took control of the air waves and warned the people via television in all languages and dialects, "My friends all over this Earth, this so called 'End of the World' could certainly happen. We are well on that path with the recent global financial meltdown and the global climate changes—changes brought about by a mistaken global concept that it is our God-given right not only to have dominion over all life on this planet, but also to abuse and misuse animals, plants and each other. As a result of this mistaken global concept, we have come to a place of massive disregard for life itself, plants, trees, water, fish, dolphins, whales and yes, billions of people. This global concept, of course, includes the mistaken belief that it is our God-given right to exploit our beautiful live organism, Earth: the waters, the earth itself and the sky. It is the mistaken belief that this is okay because Mother Earth in her unlimited capacity will absorb anything and everything and still retain her environmental integrity. Regarding our atmosphere, just look at what our ignorance has brought us. For example, do you know that it takes two tons of jet fuel for a jet liner to lift off and reach its orbital path of 30,000 - 40,000 feet, and then another two tons to land the jet. Multiply that by 10,000 jets flying over the

Pacific at any given time. The ugly truth is that this planet, the environment and all life on it are past the point of no return. By seeding and growing our global thoughts with false beliefs, the Illuminati with its dark negative use of energy will have achieved its goal: the destruction of Earth and all life on Earth."

Angelica interrupted David to tell Earth's people, "But wait! You are Spiritual Light Beings and you, like us, are travelers in this universe. I know a handful of you remember your last voyage, but I assure you that your time does not need to end. Do you think for one second that Creation would make manifest trillions and trillions of solar systems and out of these trillions of solar systems only one planet could support intelligent life? That's absurd and you know it. Scientists say that there are more than 100,000 solar systems in the Milky Way galaxy alone which support life. Multiply this by billions of galaxies and see for yourself how ridiculous it is to believe you are the only intelligent life in the universe. As you know, we've been here for some time and we're from a planet 500 light years away."

Then looking up and to the left as if accessing her memory Angelica continued, "By the way, you may remember a news flash from CNN on December 6th, 2011. It reported that the Keplar telescope located a planet in space that is habitable because it has the qualities necessary to sustain life, such as a temperature of 23 degrees Celsius. They named this planet Kepler-22b. The other important thing about this particular report was the planet's location. Kepler-22b is located 600 light years from Earth in the Lyra system. Well guess what, that just happens to be the original home world of the Pleiadians. Fancy that!"

Dream #29, March 29, 2009
Love Prevails with David
and his Father

Raymond, let's turn the storyline to David and his father. They need to resolve their issues.

Pierre and David decided to meet at the park in Berkeley. Pierre was very angry with his son because of his recent activities with the one percent. He said to David, "Did you think we wouldn't find out? By the way, did you think your laboratory plot with Sandy's friends would go unnoticed? David you have to stop these insane plans before you get yourself killed."

David grabbed his father by the shoulder, spun him around and snapped out at his dad, "Why should I listen to you? And who is the 'we' you give your allegiance to over the lives of your own wife and son? By the way, what is your connection with the Illuminati?"

At this point Pierre was quite desperate. He decided that he must come clean with his son.

Pierre tried desperately to find the right words to explain his actions. Not being very successful, he decided to tell the truth. "You see David, when you were very young you started to exhibit some very unusual abilities. You were extremely gifted, a genius, and you posed a serious threat to the power structures of the Illuminati. I did everything I could to prevent them from harming you and perhaps even killing you. The truth is, David, that I sold my soul to the Illuminati. I agreed to build them a city in an underground cavern. I also agreed to build a base shield device that would protect them from the Black Hole."

Pierre moved closer to David, held his hands and looked directly into his eyes. His voice softened and he felt great remorse as he said, "David, part of my bargain with Abernethy includes that you will be one of the agreed upon people to be saved when the rest of the world is destroyed." Then his voice rose a little and got sharper as he sternly warned his son, "David, you must stop your plans to help humanity or I won't be able to help you any longer and you and Sandy will be assassinated."

David pushed his father away and responded forcefully, "I would rather die than cooperate with those evil people!"

Breathing deeply, David moved closer to his father. He put his hands on his father's shoulders, focused in on his eyes, and said, "Dad, we have a plan—a plan that will save humanity and earth."

Pierre slowly sat down. He heard the conviction and power in David's voice. Pierre said to David, "I think I can get your message to the President. He is most interested in what Angelica and your people are doing and of course that includes you."

As for you, please David, you and Sandy must go into hiding."

David pleaded with his father, "Dad, let me awaken you so you can be saved."

Pierre moved away feeling defeated. He said, "David I don't deserve peace and I certainly don't deserve your love. Not after what I have done to protect the Illuminati. Now, you must go David."

David did not give up. He walked over to his father, put his hands on his temples, looks into his eyes and said, "Dad I see God in you."

Pierre broke down and wept.

David whispered to his father, "Dad, do you believe that you are a Spirit Being having this amazing human experience?"

Pierre answered, "Yes, of course I do."

David responded, "Dad, in a moment you will begin to feel a little bit strange and quite wonderful."

Startled, his father questioned David, "Son, what have you done?

David smiled at his dad. He said, "Dad, you have just awakened your Quantum Love Gene."

Pierre stumbled onto a chair. He said, "I feel a little weird." He looked at his son and said, "This is a good thing right?"

"Yes, Dad, this is a very good thing!"

Pierre was suddenly aware of his situation with the Illuminati. He exclaimed, "Oh, my God! What have I done?"

David held his father's hands and said, "Dad it is passed. It is now. It is important to forgive yourself and move on."

Pierre responded, "You are very wise. Yes, my Son, you are right! I love you Son. Now go before I get all teary again."

Dream #30, March 30, 2009
Merchants of Death

Angelica comes into my dreams again, and I start writing as fast as I can even as I slip into the dream.

Angelica told David, "The Illuminati are busy meeting with some military people. Although they make billions in profits by their sales of arms to warring countries, the arms dealers who are owned and controlled by the Illuminati are trying to save their livelihood. Nothing is more sinister than that. These merchants of death intentionally create an imbalance of power in order to sell more weapons to each side—all in the name of Peace, when the real sinister ugly side of capitalism is money. However, right now the entire arms-dealing enterprise is highly frustrated, divided and on edge. Because of this crack in their armor, all conversations between any of these Merchants of Death are being heard and seen by thousands of humans and visitors from Pleiades. These conversations are heard all over the world in every language.

David replied to Angelica, "Of course these conversations are broadcast simultaneously on global networks via satellites ... in *all* languages and dialects."

"Oh wait!" Sara interjected, "I'm getting an interesting conversation from what appears to be the military silo—the one located 300 feet below earth where they are housing an intercontinental missile. The conversation is coming from two men. It seems they are

American soldiers. I'm tuning in. I'll rebroadcast this so the Chinese and the whole world can hear and see it. Oh My! The Chinese already responded. They are preparing to launch their own intercontinental missiles aimed at three USA targets: Los Angeles, NYC and the largest military base in the US—Norfolk, Virginia. Here are the voice conversations rebroadcast on all televisions. This information is now 1.5 minutes old."

General Chang and eight missile experts, especially trained for underground silo defense preparedness, live down in the silo without seeing the sky or Sun light for a rotation period of 30 days. These eight men have been selected from a pool of 10,000 qualified soldiers. Although these men have trained extensively in simulation sessions and exercises, including any foreseeable event, the real thing seems a lot more dangerous, stressful and scary.

General Chang has just heard on TV that the Americans had managed to manually launch three missiles toward China even though the Pleiadians had jammed the frequencies. This silo located near Shanghai is the latest version of intercontinental ballistic missiles capable of reaching the coastal targets in the US.

The mood down in the Shanghai silo was very tense.

China's General Chang said to Lieutenant Wong, "Yes I know the Americans have launched three missiles aimed at our country. We saw it on television via these foreigners from who knows where. We too have this ability. We can bypass the jamming devices they have imposed on us. We can do it manually."

Lieutenant Wong said to his subordinates, "We are blind down here. We cannot send or receive voice or video signals to our superiors. Let's ask the computer. Punch in, 'Situation Blind'. Look, the computer is responding: 'open file, follow prompts and execute.'"

Lieutenant Wong issued a sharp command to his subordinate Staff Sergeant Deng sitting next to him, "Staff Sergeant Deng open the file REM. It's Response for Emergency Measures (REM)."

Staff Sergeant Deng replied, "Sir, yes Sir," and typed in the file name. It flashed REM on all monitors in the room in bright red very large letters. A loud annoying alarm bounced off the walls of the small sound-proof room.

General Chang yelled, "Will someone turn that dammed alarm off?"

Staff Sergeant Deng reached over to a separate panel where the large red button was flashing with the word REM and hit the button with much more force than required. The room became absolutely still. Not a sound could be heard. The large red letters REM were still flashing. The room was filled with six very startled, frightened men.

General Chang yelled, "Attention!" whereupon they all came to their senses and snapped to attention. General Chang walked by each of his hand-picked officers, looked each one in the eyes and said, "Each one of you was picked by me. You were selected from a pool of one hundred men. They were selected from one thousand men, and they in turn were selected from

10,000 applicants. You have earned the right to be here. You are the best of the best. This is a critical moment for all of us—a moment to test the best. I have the utmost faith in each and every one of you."

General Chang then turned to Staff Sergeant Deng and asked him to read the Instructions. Deng read, "REM means Response for Emergency Measures. State the situation."

General Chang stared at the monitor, then turned to Deng and instructed him to type the following, word for word, "We are unable to send or receive any communication from our superiors."

The room was deadly silent—everyone was waiting for the computer to respond. It seemed like a lifetime, but in fact only a moment had passed. In big bold red letters they saw written on the screen: *in this scenario the programmed response from the Chinese Central High Command is to assume an eminent attack and respond in kind.*

"Yes" said Lieutenant Wong, "I understand your orders and agree, but this will start a third world war. How long can we survive down here? The air up top will be heavy with radioactive dust storms for many years."

General Chang said, "Something tells me that our new visitors will not let this happen. After all, these Aliens have control of the entire global military telecommunication systems everywhere on earth. Nonetheless, this limited response is a defensive strategy against an aggressive military action by the United States who has already launched missiles against us."

General Chang continued, "I repeat, as senior officer I say we must respond no matter what our chances of survival. We cannot launch electronically—everything is jammed ... but we can launch mechanically."

Staff Sgt. Lee emerged from his post in engineering and said, "General Chang Sir, permission to speak freely, Sir."

General Chang nodded his head in approval, saying, "You know, I have always expected all of you to express yourselves and your opinions are of value to me.

Staff Sgt. Lee said, "Don't you think it's a little strange, that we are getting all our Intel from the TV broadcasted from the aliens? How do we know for sure, the Americans have launched three missiles at us? Sir. I am against any retaliation based on unproven information.

At this point three other officers joined Staff Sgt. Lee. A very loud argument ensued. Guns were drawn and shots fired. Many rapid shots were heard. Three men were down. Lee, Chang and Wong remained alive in a stand-off pointing guns at each other. General Chang, the most senior officer said with a very shaky yet commanding tense voice, "We must launch these missiles—the US missiles are already five minutes into launch."

As the Chinese prepared to launch their missiles, the Americans, trapped in their bunkers far beneath the Earth, could see and hear, via television signals, what the Chinese were preparing … just the same as the Chinese were seeing and listening to the Americans. So both the Chinese and Americans were able to see and hear each other. The Chinese knew that the Americans had launched three missiles aimed at the Chinese, and the Americans knew the Chinese were preparing to launch three missiles at the USA.

Of course, what was happening between the Chinese and Americans was all orchestrated and controlled by the Illuminati. The Illuminati's goal was to start a war between the US and China and blame it on the Aliens!

The Chinese officers remaining alive were of all ages. General Chang commanded with an intimidating voice of authority giving evidence of his thirty years of military experience, "Launch missiles! Each of us will launch one missile mechanically. It will take about five minutes. That means the American missiles will be ten minutes down range."

General Chang then paused as he remembered that the whole world could see him live on television. He said, "Okay, wait a minute. Everyone all over the world heard and saw all this and live coverage continues? Never mind, we have a right and a responsibility to defend China. We can't communicate with our superiors. We are in charge. Article 382a of our standing orders stipulates that 'When faced with armed missiles fired upon our homeland and we are incommunicado, our orders are to respond according order 1011.27a of the standing orders.' So we are in the right. We have the responsibility to defend our country!

and the computer has confirmed this."

Angelica asserted herself into the broadcast to the whole world including the Chinese, "We can and will disarm and destroy the American missiles. We need three minutes."

General Chang can I have an emergency teleconference between you and your president Mr. Hu Lintao? Oh! Don't worry. The line is open as of now."

General Chang hastily agreed. He typed a few orders on his ipad3. Moments later President Hu Lintao appeared on his iPad and General Chang said, "Greetings Mr. President."

President Lintao returned the greeting with a slight bow to his trusted general.

General Chang continued, "Mr. President, we are in conference with the leader of our visitors, the Pleiadians. Her name is Angelica."

After introductions were made, Angelica asked David to take over. David said, "Mr. President Hu Lintao, I have asked General Chang for three minutes delay in your rightful duty to respond to three US missiles on their way to your country. We ask for your approval. Time is of the essence. Let me add Sir, these new friends are 100 thousand years ahead of us in development. Together we can neutralize the US missiles in seconds. Mr. President, the whole world is watching and its survival depends on your response."

There was a pause, then the Chinese President Lintao said, "General Chang what do you make of this awkward situation?"

General Chang responded, "Sir, let's give them

three minutes. If the US missiles are still airborne in three and a half minutes, we will launch our counter attack against the US."

President Hu Lintao turned to Angelica and asked, "Can you stop these missiles?"

Angelica responded, "Yes, absolutely. There will be no nuclear radiation as the bombs will merely be changed into a harmless substance. I have to tell you that if you launch your missiles they too will be transformed into harmless material and redirected to the ocean."

President Hu Lintao gave his okay saying, "Yes, do it! And thank you so much. Angelica, the whole world is in your debt."

Thirty seconds went by. The Pleiadians had the coordinates of the three missiles and their trajectories. They were 40,000 feet up and moving at 3,000 miles per hour. As per the plan two Pleiadians would tackle each of the three missiles. It would take us less than thirty seconds to reach them and two minutes to dispose of them—that's a total of two and half minutes.

The communication was all broadcast live on TVs all over the world ... well almost. As David was talking he was traveling toward the missiles at 20,000 km per minute. He reported back, "We are almost there. Yes, I see them and my five Pleiadian Sisters are here. The missiles are about 500 meters apart. We have reached the missiles ... twenty seven seconds have passed. Now all of us are concentrating on the changing of the nuclear material—the bombs, into an inert harmless material. Actually, the process is very simple. We consciously see the molecules and then the atoms. Focusing our Quantum Love power we are able to vibrate our energy at the same frequency as the molecular molecules. Once we are tuned into the same frequency, we can change the molecular structure to whatever, in this case, lead."

There, *we did it!* We changed the bombs on all three missiles to lead. Two minutes have gone by. Okay, time to drop the missiles into the Atlantic Ocean. Indeed, they are now aimed at the ocean. We are now pushing the missiles at 20,000 km/per hour. In 5, 4, 3, 2, 1, 0 seconds and they have disappeared into the Atlantic—in total two minutes and fifty nine seconds have gone by."

Meanwhile, the Chinese were still preparing to launch their missiles with their fingers on the "on" switch. Then they heard David's words, "Yes, the US missiles have crashed into the ocean."

I look at the pen. My hand is shaking. I put the pen down with great difficulty. It does not seem to want to let go of my fingers. I am emotionally drained, I think to myself how many more of these dreams can I take? I think I will lie down and have a rest.

Dream #31, March 31, 2009
Abernathy Shows his True Colors

Pierre Chartrand was in his office in the underground shelter he had built for the Illuminati. He had secretly set the reactors to overload ten minutes after he went top side and out of harm's way.

Abernathy walked in, followed by three security guards armed with p-90s. He said to Pierre, "I understand you have been talking with the President about spreading this so-called Love Gene. Did you really think we would not find out about it?"

Pierre smiled sarcastically and retorted, "I was thinking that you would find out about it after passing through the Black Hole, and then you would all turn into good guys!"

Abernathy was not amused. He snapped his fingers, and a guard raised his p-90 assault weapon and squeezed the trigger for just two seconds. A stream of bullets was set on their way to a close-by target. Pierre was hit with a dozen or more bullets as he jerked back, slammed against the wall behind him and then fell to the floor in a pool of blood with at least ten bullets to his chest. Moments later the room was filled with a bright white light focused on Pierre lying on the floor. The light disappeared and all that was left on the floor was the bullet-ridden clothes and no Pierre. Abernathy was absolutely stunned. He fell to his knees, and for the first time in a life of crime began to doubt his chosen career.

Dream #32, April 1, 2009
David and his Five Pleiadian Super Women are Honored

"Remember Raymond," says Angelica, "the Chinese were about to respond in the last dream."

I look up at Angelica and say, "I'm both excited and afraid. I don't like violence and this looks very serious."

"Yes, I understand", says Angelica, "just remember this is a message in story form by you and from me."

The Chinese sent out the following message over the airways, "We will stand down. President Lintao will listen to your plan. Here is the President of China. He wishes to address the whole world."

The Chinese President, Mr. Hu Lintao said, "To my people, congratulations on your willingness to obey orders and do your duty. And thank you for listening and making the correct decision. There will be no work today. Whoever you are, Angelica, we are most interested in your plan."

To the USA, please know this, your people followed orders. For that you must thank them. We are both guilty of one major error. That error is in believing that we are enemies. The only enemy is the Illuminati whose entire existence is the perpetuation ignorance, fear and distrust. This experience marks a new and very important step toward lasting peace."

As if on a roll, President Mr. Hu Lintao continued speaking to the world, "With the help of our Pleiadian ancestors, Earth will survive man's ignorance and the pending alignment of our solar system with the center of our galaxy where I understand there exists a Black Hole rapidly approaching Earth. I will strongly encourage my people to vote yes to the assistance of our Pleiadian ansestors."

Very happy with this announcement David replied, "Thank you President Hu Lintao. Today you made a historical decision. For this the world is indeed grateful. Now we turn to Ms. Castrorez, President of the USA."

President Castrorez said, "Thank you to David and the five Pleiadian women who helped David disarm and destroy the missiles. These missiles our brave soldiers launched in good conscience while executing their orders. It is very easy to justify our expressions of aggression that were based on fear of a falsely perceived enemy—the Chinese! It's become clear to me that the real culprit is the Illuminati whose entire agenda is the dark negative use of energy. Now to the President of China, Mr. Hu Lintao, please accept my sincere gratitude for your decision to trust our Pleiadian Visitors. From today forward the world will never be the same."

"To my Chinese neighbors on this tiny ship we call Earth, I say this, 'I believe it is time to lay down our fears and embrace the truth about *who* and *what* we are: Spirit-Light Beings having this amazing experience incarnated in Human form. Today we are visited by our true mentors, David and his friends from Pleiades. As I speak, both science and religious communities all over this planet are facing the awesome task of coming to grips with this event. God bless our tiny precious planet. God (Hunab Ku) bless the planet Pleiades.'"

President Castrorez caught his breath and then said emphatically, "Today I accept the indisputable fact that we are Pleiadian. Our visitors/mentors from Pleiades also recognize Hunab Ku, the Mayan's name for God—creator of all that is."

The facts speak for themselves. Today we were seen on TV all over the planet simultaneously as we averted a global war by using technology and inter-Planetary cooperation such as we have only witnessed in the movies. This is truly the most incredible event of humankind. Something tells me we are about to experience more of this awesome power as the Black Hole approaches the center of our Galaxy."

I believe these Beings are here to help—no—rather to save us from our present course of self-destruction. I understand their help is subject to an agreement by all nations and the meeting regarding this agreement is about to take place on the Pleiadian ship called Starship Cosmos."

Again to David and the Pleiadians, on behalf of the United States of America, I, as President of the United States, humbly extend to you our deepest gratitude."

Dream #33, April 2, 2009
Meeting of Minds on the
Mother Ship Starship Cosmos

Again over the air waves, Angelica talked to everyone about Starship Cosmos, "First, let's share a word about this awesome huge ship Starship Cosmos. She has some interesting qualities. Starship Cosmos is about 5 kilometers long (3.5 miles), about 3.5 kilometers at the widest point (2.0 miles) and about 3.5 kilometers high (2.0 miles) ... the size of Stanley Park or perhaps Central Park. By far her most interesting attribute is that she is an organic ship. That's right! Starship Cosmos is alive! In appearance she is shaped like a big snail. Starship Cosmos can support 500,000 people and is powered by our Suns. She is highly intelligent and communicates with her crew by very advanced telepathic thought processes. But let's not forget that we Pleiadians live in what we call the fifth or sixth and even eighth dimension so communicating with this wonderful ship is no trouble. Starship Cosmos is Light Energy. Her mode of travel is EMP love energy (electro-magnetic pulse engine) which is used primarily for atmospheric travel. For pure Divine love power and for inter-planetary travel Starship Cosmos can travel the speed of thought teleportation. To put this into perspective, Starship Cosmos can travel thousands of times faster than the speed of light which is186,000 miles per second."

Onboard Starship Cosmos, President of the UN, Mr. Noble said to the members of the UN, "In a very short time *all* heads of countries all over the world will meet on the mother ship Starship Cosmos with these Pleiadian Beings. Please understand that our survival and the well-being of our entire six billion inhabitants is dependent on how we use the most powerful gift we have been given at conception, and that is volition. Volition is the innate gift given to all Sentient Beings to be able to make choices. Today and in the next few days we will have a very profound choice to make. The question we need to ask ourselves is this, 'Will I make this decision based on the old way of fear, or will it be based on the new way of mutual respect and love? For some this will require the release of a very old belief of the concept of enemies. For others who are less likely to be dictated to by traditions thousands of years old, the decision to accept the assistance offered by the Pleiadians will be easy."

Angelica said, "Thank you Mr. President of the UN, Mr. Noble. That was most inspiring. We will get back to the Starship Cosmos meeting in just a minute."

At the beginning of the next dream, Angelica says to me, "Raymond, tonight in your dream state, I will talk about the global financial giants and their power and control over human affairs."

Dream #34, April 3, 2009
Global Giants of the Financial
Meetings ... in Secret of Course

Angelica continued, "Meanwhile let's see what the global financial giants are up to. I'm sure all this Oneness love talk and talk about ascension is creating a very upsetting experience in the ranks of the secret Illuminati. Their plan to pit the US against their falsely perceived enemy the Chinese did not go off as planned. They need to regroup and look ... sure enough there is a secret meeting taking place. Now, mind you, it is not being held in a plush hotel in the Caribbean, rather its down, way down two kilometers underground. Their meeting appears to be held in a special subterranean city-like mansion built for their use only. This very large mansion was built by Pierre Chartrand under duress and blackmail from Abernathy's group."

As Angelica spoke, the Pleiadian undercover agent and shape shifter named Gloria was making her way down to the underground meeting place of the Illuminati. She was appearing as Mr. Don Brown, Security Chief of the five hundred man plain clothes force. Mr. Brown had been teleported to a secured location above ground. He was in suspended animation for the duration of Gloria's mission in the Illuminati subterranean huge mansion.

As Gloria approached the meeting place she reported to David, telepathically, "This place is very big. It is not surprising that they need a massive amount of man power in order to keep paranoia in check—particularly given that they function entirely with negative dark energy."

Angelica informed her global TV audience, "Gloria/Dan Brown has access to just about everything everywhere. Her telepathic abilities are astounding even in Pleiadian standards. She is very capable of transmitting massive amounts of incriminating evidence she has gathered during her stay here for the past six months. The data is sent telepathically to David and his team aboard Starship Cosmos. They in turn are rebroadcasting the data to nearly every TV in the world. The data is uncensored and unedited."

In every spoken language and dialect, Angelica transmitted to the world via TV her communication from Gloria regarding Gloria's observations of the secret meeting place. Gloria said, "It has ten elevators. These elevators are really something else. Even in the known standards they travel at an incredible speed up and down the two kilometer ride to the home of the rich and the elite, and they are huge with a cargo capacity of at least ten midsize American cars. In human standards it's just amazing! The shelter/city is at least 40 square kilometers and is lit up like it was above ground. There is a transit system containing at least 5,000 lite rail cars. There are at least 200,000—fully equipped suites and hundreds of large meeting rooms. The Sub City has everything including 20 swimming pools and very large recreational centers each equipped with every conceivable amenity known to man. It's just like being topside in the USA. For shopping there are five 40,000-square-foot malls. There are also ten hospitals fully equipped and better than any on the surface and the list goes on. How many people will this house you might ask?

Angelica continued, explaining, "Working with Chief Gloria/Brown are ten changelings and telepaths. They are also shape shifters—that means they can be anybody anywhere, anytime. Most of them can hear and see everything thus giving the whole world the advantage of knowing what the Illuminati are planning! Gloria says that you would be absolutely flabbergasted to know who is actually down there—she says that it is like a 'who's who list' including many top leaders of the financial and political world. And guess who paid for it all? The answer is military sales, profits from the drug cartels and of course the funneled tax dollars from the middle class all over the world."

Angelica continued with her broadcast, "Now, I say to the Earth global community, let's see and hear what the Illuminati are secretly meeting about. You can watch it on channel 01, or on the Internet. We will broadcast the report in every language and dialect."

These meetings reflect the thirteen-member organization of the group which controls ninety nine percent of Earth's financial wealth. Needless to say, they are not aware of our presence."

Let's find out what the dark side is up to, but before we do that let me give you a little more background information. This facility is two kilometers underground near what has come to be known as *AREA*

51. It is a military base—a remote detachment of Edwards Air Force Base. It is located in the southern portion of Nevada in western USA. This Illuminati hideout is equipped with the Earth's most sophisticated telecommunication installations. Because the Illuminati can do, to a much lesser extent, what the Pleiadians are doing; i.e., jamming and controlling all satellites and ground stations, they honestly believe they can fight back and control the telecommunications and the US military complex. So, when the Illuminati arrive and *secure themselves* in the mini environment and try to turn their communication systems on they will be in for a big surprise! Let's listen to what they are saying in their secret meeting!"

Mr. Roughchild, the President of the Illuminati, said to his second-in-command, Charlotte, representing the royalty of England, "Have our engineers initiate all global satellites. It is time someone shows those Alien invaders who is boss on Earth. Charlotte, shall we have our media staff man get our television studio ready for broadcast?

"Yes, but first let's tune into American television and see what's happening." Charlotte continued, "We will be up and running and tuned in within one minute."

Angelica then focused in on Gloria who had shape shifted and now looked like the chief of communications, Mr. Chang Ling. While Mr. Chang Ling responded to the command of Charlotte, Gloria turned on the massive generators to full capacity making sure everything was working.

Back at the Pleiadians headquarters (which by the

way is in geo-sync orbit with 10,000 other ships 2,000 km above Earth), both Angelica and David were monitoring the Illuminati meeting.

Angelica said, "At the right time we are preparing to jam all their transmissions. Because we plan to use Pleiadian power and technology, which is thousands of years more advanced than anything on Earth, we can easily control any computer and communication systems anywhere ... including the Illuminati's sophisticated state of the art one hundred billion dollar installation with their private satellites."

Back with the Illuminati Charlotte said, "President Roughchild, we are ready to turn on our communication system."

President Roughchild replied, "OK, turn it on."

Charlotte: "Mr. Roughchild, we are live. Here is a TV transmission from FOX."

Please remember, the Pleiadians have 100% control of all communications on Earth. The Illuminati are led to believe they can transmit and receive at their own discretion, but in fact it is only because the Pleiadians allow it to happen.

President Castrorez was speaking, "Please understand our survival and well-being ... "

Roughchild: "Number One, prepare the media group to activate Studio A and get me a direct line to President Castrorez. I'll let him know who is in charge of this game."

Angelica: "Do we have a live feed from the Illuminati? Oh good! There, we have it … . Now let it run. Don't let them know yet. Don't jam any of their transmissions or receiving of TV. We want the entire world to get this transmission on their TV's."

Charlotte speaking to her assistant, Mark: "Mark, get me President Castrorez."

Mark: "Yes, Mam. Right away! Mam, President Castrorez is on your red private line."

Charlotte: "Mr. Roughchild, the President of the USA is on your red line."

Roughchild: "Mr. President, this is Robert Roughchild. How are you, Mr. President?"

Castrorez: "Robert, good of you to call. I take it you are well situated."

Roughchild: "Yes, Mr. President, We are all well situated. Mr. President we need to talk. Is this a secure line? You know what I mean?"

Castrorez: "Well, given the present circumstances it is best you know that any and all conversations we have will be monitored."

Roughchild: "Well, Mr. President, I'm confident that our people have control and therefore we can be assured that we have a secure line. The thing of it is, Barack, we need to agree on a principle of mutual cooperation to the benefit of our interests, don't you agree?"

President Castrorez: "Mr. Roughchild, every word I speak here is being heard and watched by the people of the USA and the world."

Mr. Roughchild raised his voice said in a razor sharp tone, "Let us remind you, Sir, of our control and power over all global economic and political affairs. You really don't think these Aliens scare us, do you?"

Castrorez: "Well Robert, I think this: You and your organization and your ninety nine percent grip on planetary financial and political control is in fact coming to a grinding halt. I know this is not what you wanted to hear."

Mr. Roughchild: "Mr. President, I would have thought by now you had a better understanding of our historical power over the past 8,000 years. I'm very disappointed in your desire to capitulate to these Alien bastards. Understand that we intend to place all your US assets in harm's way against these foreign invaders. We will crush your own assets with your American military. That's right Mr. President. We will activate control over your mighty power. Before this conversation ends all your forces will be responding to my orders. To show legitimacy, they will be using your name and office. Get this straight, without us Mr. President, you have no power!"

Castrorez: "Robert, you know if we had had this conversation three days ago I would have agreed because it is true all global financial events are, or should I say *were,* under your control. But now, Robert, I am absolutely happy to tell you, Sir, that your power is useless as of this very moment—you and your ultimate expression of greed and power have come to an end. The good news is—you can watch it all on television."

Mark: "Excuse me Mr. Roughchild ... ."

Mr. Roughchild: "Not now Mark. Charlotte, shut him up *now*!"

Charlotte: "Yes Sir!" She drew her gun and shot Mark dead.

Mr. Roughchild: "Now, where were we ... . Oh yes, Power—wait a minute Charlotte. What the hell is going on? Why have I not heard from our people in Washington...the military Generals?"

Charlotte: "Sir, we are not able to get out. We cannot transmit. Someone or something is jamming our signals. Wait, I think one may have gotten through. It's a submarine off the coast of Iceland. But Sir, we have no direct Intelligence as to the location, or who our enemies are."

Mr. Roughchild: "Our enemies are very clear. All this nonsense about Alien control is being orchestrated by the Chinese. Order whatever military assets you can from the Sub against Beijing and other military targets in China."

Mr. Roughchild back to Barack Castrorez: "Mr. President, this conversation is ended. By the way, so is your presidency."

President Castrorez: "Robert, you really should turn on your television and tune into channel 01!"

Meanwhile Mr. Bob Roughchild, the most ruthless leader ever in power of the Illuminati, had made contact with Captain Rick Chaney of the US submarine named Bucktail—she is a US nuclear missile-carrying submarine off the coast of Iceland. This submarine was somehow overlooked by the Pleiadians and so remained undetected. Mr. Roughchild said to Captain Chaney, "Rick, my boy, I need you to do a small favor for me."

Rick responded, "Hi Bob. How the hell are you?"

Roughchild said to Chaney, "Rick; Rick shut up and listen! I need for you to launch all your missiles. By the way, how many nukes do you have?"

Rick answered, "Three."

Roughchild said, "Great! Launch them all at the biggest Chinese Cities. Do it now!"

Chainy replied, "You got it Bob! Are we at war Bob?"

There was no answer. Chainy ended by saying, "You owe me one, Bob"

Click, and the phone went dead.

Dream #35, April 4, 2009
the Pleiadian Powers Demonstrated

Angelica reported, "We have already dispatched a small team of Pleiadian teleporters. As I speak this desperate attempt by the most powerful evil organization is being disabled and neutralized. Yes, I'm getting both visual and audio from our Pleiadian secret service agent named Nancy.

Nancy: "We are approaching the US missiles. Two other Pleiadians and I have teleported aboard three US missiles which are on a trajectory heading toward Beijing, Shanghai and Hong Kong, China. You can see the three US missiles as we approach China via my video feed. Look ... right before our eyes we are witnessing the molecular structure of the warheads being changed. There we have it! We have successfully disarmed the war heads and converted the nuclear material to an inert non radio-active material. These missiles were intercepted just three kilometers off the coast of China, that is, about thirty seconds from impact. I am happy to officially report they are now dead in the water."

Roughchild: "Damn. What the hell is going on here? We have total control over the affairs of Mankind. We have been in control for more than 8,000 years. Would somebody please tell me what's happening? Yes, I did see it all on television. Damn disgusting! Our planet is being invaded by Aliens and we are too damn blind and soft to see it. Those damn

Democrats and bleeding hearts in Europe and Washington are brainwashed by these Alien invaders. What's to come of us? Our blood line is pure. Our New World Order will prevail! We will dominate the entire planet in all areas. Through and by our leadership we will make a new world—a world with order and with complete obedience to our new rules of justice. For thousands of years we have ruled the whole world while its people have been going about their business as if in a coma—blindly ignorant of us."

Someone in the background was yelling at Roughchild and he responded, "Damn it, can't you see I'm on a roll? What is it?"

Charlotte: "Sir, I think you should see Channel 01. It is you Sir on Global TV."

Roughchild: "Oh! My Lucifer! You mean all over the globe?"

Charlotte: "Yes Sir, all over the globe."

Roughchild: "And all of the missiles … ?"

Charlotte: "Sir, they were destroyed by people or something looking like people. We all see and hear you—me, everyone. How is this possible Sir? I thought we … ."

Roughchild: "Enough! Turn it off! From now on we will conduct our meeting in writing only!"

Angelica says to me at the beginning of Dream #36, "We will talk about the Vatican tonight."

Dream #36, April 5, 2009
The Vatican

David reported Live on Channel 01, "We are getting some interesting reactions to our presence from the Vatican—the seat of the Roman Catholic Church. We are intercepting what appears to be a meeting of the Pope with his cardinals from around the world. This will be of particular interest to the Catholic membership of about 1.2 billion followers. I am not sure if the Vatican knows we can hear and see their Secret meeting."

You all know me as David and you know that I have been appointed ambassador to the Inter Galactic Federation of Planets as represented here on Earth by the Pleiadians of the Star System Pleiades. My mission in this moment is to reassure all of you that the Pleiadians among us have only one goal. This goal is to assist us as our solar system moves into alignment with the center of our galaxy and the Black Hole. This event will happen on Earth as well as on a galactic scale. It will happen to everyone. At this time, you must make a choice. Eighty percent of the entire population of Earth must vote 'Yes' to our assistance in order for Earth to survive the Black Hole. The Black Hole is only hours away. If you vote 'Yes,' and thereby accept that you are Spirit Light Beings incarnated in human form, your QL Gene (Quantum Love Gene) that has been dormant for some 10,000 years will automatically be activated. Upon activation you will be uplifted into the fifth dimension. For those of you who choose to believe that you are human beings rather than Spirit Beings, you will perish."

David then went on to explain to the people, "Please understand that a metaphysical, quantum paradigm shift will take place as we pass through the whirling disc at the center of the Black Hole and ascension will occur. Life will continue without further interruption from me or the Pleiadians. Having said this, we will also assist you to make a course correction."

Angelica added to what David had said. She reminded the people, "We Pleiadians intend to help Earth leaders—leaders like Castrorez of the US, President Hu Jitao of China and all other leaders of governments. This is a huge opportunity for all societies on Earth to regain control over your global socio-economic and political systems. The choice is up to you. Please understand this: ninety-nine percent of your people up until today have been asleep, i.e., hypnotized to the drum beat of a global economy which depends entirely on consumer spending. A similar phenomenon happened 10,000 years ago when we, your Pleiadian ancestors, had already been present on Earth for 12,000 years."

Excited, David interrupted Angelica and explained, "This time, however, stock markets call the global hypnotizing machine the 'consumer index' and through this consumer index the Illuminati keep us active in our consumer addiction. We are fortunate to have the presence of Light Beings here with us today in real time—Light Beings who are in fact our ancestors willing to help us *wake up*! As I have already said, the Pleiadians are exceptional, gentle Beings and are at least 100,000 years more advanced than we are. Believe me when I tell you that they need absolutely nothing from us. I don't mean to sound repetitious, but the plain truth is that the Pleiadians colonized this planet 26,000 years ago and now here we are. They want only to help us move through this inevitable planet change in a way that we can continue our evolution on a planet safe from climate destruction and the loss of untold human lives ... to live in a world ruled by peace and love that is free of nuclear weapons."

Angelica spoke, "Thank you David. Repetition is always good. If there is anything more you inhabitants of Earth need to hear and see to prove to you who we truly are, we Pleiadians will make it available to you."

Dream #37, April 6, 2009
Planetary Reaction:
the World Response

An unnamed news reporter on BNN News spoke, "We are getting mixed reactions from all over the planet. There is considerable rioting and panic in the streets. In most major cities people are grappling with this unbelievable event. It seems that people from the major religions, such as the Christians, Jews and Muslims, are really shaken up. The thought of their God-based spiritual beliefs being challenged by the presence of these highly advanced 'peace-loving' Beings from the planet called Pleiades is overwhelming. This challenge forces people of these major religions to think outside the box of Genesis, and of course threatens the foundation of their core beliefs by which they have lived for 2,000 years."

David added to what the news reporter had just said, "There is one very important point that I may not have made clear. Earth is part of a huge dimensional shift taking place in our galaxy. By virtue of being an inhabitant here on Earth you will partake in this dimensional shift, and you have a choice to make this evolutionary leap forward or to perish. That is why these Beings, our very own ancestors of a super advanced race, are here. Again, I repeat, they are here solely for the purpose of assisting Earth's many diverse cultures to make these transitions peacefully and perhaps even joyfully. I know the transitions' go against two-thirds of our population's religious beliefs. Perhaps this reminder will help: remember that the Creator created the entire universe—not just earth and our solar system. They are not here to change or threaten any religious beliefs; yet, you need to know that Galactic consciousness rising is already happening. Experiencing a higher consciousness, the evolutionary jump becomes possible. Not everyone will be ready to embrace this incredible evolutionary jump, and that is okay. No matter what your decision is, the Pleiadians will honor your decision," David reassured the people listening to BNN News.

Angelica on BNN News: "In 24 hours Earth time, at 12 noon tomorrow, more than 13,000 leaders from all over your planet will meet on our mother ship we call Starship Cosmos. They will meet with me and 10,000 other Pleiadians and David. All of Earth's people will be able to watch and hear our meeting. It will be broadcast on more than 3000 channels and in all languages. The meeting will be interactive—you will listen to us and we will listen to you."

Please understand that the shift has already begun. Earth is central to this galactic dimensional shift and Creation has seen fit to move this shift in alignment with Its desire. According to your particular religious theology, you might say that due to this shift you will be going to Heaven."

In simple terms, this shift helps you to recognize that each and every living soul is a part of God's

Creation, that you are a Sentient Being. Again, in case you have forgotten what being a Sentient Being means, it means you are endowed with volition—the right and ability to make choices between two or more options. Volition is the greatest gift God has given you and is an expression of selfless love. Used wisely volition provides a protective shield for the Light Energy."

Angelica continued, "The Illuminati, on the other hand, have chosen to embrace the dark negative path. You see, on Earth this gift of volition has been largely infiltrated by the dark side—the Illuminati. They invented 'divide and conquer' thousands of years ago as a means of control and since then this fear-provoking way of controlling the masses has been used by every empire."

Let's turn our attention back to what is happening. As you heard on Channel 01 a short time ago, the Illuminati leader, R. Roughchild, said that he vowed to crush the invaders. He sent three US missiles to destroy a large part of China. They were, of course, intercepted and easily neutralized by our Sisters. Roughchild wanted to start a war and blame it on us Pleiadians! They used their right of volition and deliberately chose to embrace the Dark Energy."

Dream #38, April 7, 2009
The Force/God/Hunab Ku

Angelica turns her attention to me and asks, "Raymond, are you still with me?"

I respond with a mixture of enthusiasm, anxiety and joy, "Yes!!"

Smiling Angelica says, "You have such incredible staying power. I shall continue my story. I am sure that our message will be received and understood in the movie The Quantum Love Gene that you are about to produce."

Angelica continued to remind Earth's people of the importance of volition by giving an example from the movies. "Remember in your Hollywood Sci-Fi, *Star Wars*, the Universal Intelligence is depicted as 'The Force'—it is impersonal and neutral. The Force, 'It', is the energy field that binds, stabilizes and creates worlds. 'It' is Creation, God. In the movie *Star Wars* a person chooses to be either one with the Light of The Force—goodness, love, etc., or chooses to be one with the power of the Dark Side as you saw depicted in the character Darth Vader. Well, *Star Wars* is right! The universe (God) is neutral and impersonal. If 'It' were not neutral and impersonal, you wouldn't have been given the power to choose between good and evil! The Force becomes personal when we become aware of Its Presence and Its Truth—as we become aware, we personalize The Force."

Angelica's voice softened and became more joyfully vibrant as she said almost in a whisper, "My Earth Brothers and Sisters, come along with me in imagination and imagine your *new world*. It is a world free of poverty, a world free of nuclear weapons, a world free of the concept of enemies, a world willing and able to feed its six billion people. It is a world with a socio-economic system based on co-operation, love and freedom. That's right, keep imagining with me: it is a world devoid of the need for the ego to be in control, a world devoid of diseases, a world with a pristine environment equal to the environment before the industrial revolution, a world where fossil fuels are not used anymore, a world where anyone can be anywhere anytime just by thinking about it—that's right, teleportation without machines—and much more. Oh yes! Best yet, this *new world* is a world in which fear is no longer here and the concept of an enemy is eliminated. It is a world devoid of the addiction of accumulation."

Dream #39, April 8, 2009
The Vatican and the
Gathering of Catholics

Angelica switched the attention back to the Vatican. "We understand that Pope Domenici from the Vatican is preparing to address the world. It seems the Vatican had their private meeting with their Cardinals. Nothing was said that would upset your transition. They did have a very hot, heavy, loud theological debate. Some think the Pleiadians are the devil, but most, including the Pope, think the Pleiadians are 'Bringers of the Light.' They reasoned that despite the Pleiades lack of biblical reverence that as Spirit Light Beings they possess goodness and righteous thinking. The Pope and his Cardinals have concluded this based on observing the Pleiadians words and actions."

I'm presently talking with Cardinal Louwette who is their spokesperson and speaks English. We will make the Vatican's announcement live on … yes, channel 01 in 3-2-1"

David presided over the announcements on the air.

Cardinal Louwette "Thank you. Yes, we know of all your good, honorable deeds David. The world owes you deep love and gratitude. The Pope has prepared a statement as a result of our meeting. He will deliver it to the world in just a moment. Our television Studio is setting up for the broadcast on your Channel 01. Is that Okay?"

David: "Yes, Channel 01. You may proceed on your schedule. We are monitoring your progress."

Technician (Channel 01 Technician): "Angelica, we are ready for the Pope's broadcast."

Angelica: "Pope Domenici, we are ready for your broadcast on channel 01."

Technician: "OK, in 3,2,1 ... ."

Pope: "Good evening to Roman Catholics all over the world. Good evening to all people in all countries, and also, good evening to our new visitors. To my fellow Catholics, I speak as your leader. To all Earth's people, I speak as a fellow Spirit Light Being."

We are in the midst of the event we have all been waiting for. It is described in many different ways in many religions—as 'the end of the world, Armageddon, judgment day;' however, what we call it doesn't really matter. What does concern us is that our beliefs and structures of religion are being challenged; or to put it another way, maybe the real truth is that we are faced with a very difficult unfolding of events. So to my fellow Catholics, I say this, I am shaken at the roots of my beliefs. It is not a negative experience, but rather an awakening of possibilities completely outside of the normal thinking of my religious beliefs. Facing new changes that seem inevitable, I am urging each and every one of us to turn to the love of each other and know that Jesus Christ is here with us in Spirit. Remember that fear is the Devil's work. As Catholics, it is our mission to remain calm and pray for peace, love and harmony in the face of this ending of time on Earth. Remember, you will be judged by God. Know that God has the capacity and compassion to forgive all sins. All you have to do is acknowledge your sins and be willing to repent."

The Pope continued, "I also say this to you. Please do not engage in any form of physical or verbal abuse or in any violence against anyone, including these Beings who have come in peace. They have shown no form of aggression whatsoever. They are obviously many thousands of years ahead of us in evolution. I know it is very hard to fathom a belief in alien life. But look at it this way, Angelica, on behalf of the Pleiadians, does acknowledge their belief in God, Creator of all that is. In conclusion, I see now that evolution is in fact the same as creation. In order for creation to be in constant motion, the Universe which is God, is expressing and is in fact constantly expanding. I say this to you in the name of God, the Son and the Holy Spirit. Pray to God for peace, understanding and salvation. When you vote, I urge you to choose Evolution."

Angelica: "Thank you Pope Domenici. Let me reassure you that we know and believe that there is one Universe, and one Creation by whatever name you choose to use."

Dream #40, April 9, 2009
Back to the Meeting aboard
Mother Ship, Starship Cosmos

Reporter from BNN News: "Thirteen thousand Earth Beings were teleported to the Pleiades mother ship named Starship Cosmos. Looking out from the mother ship called Starship Cosmos, Earth Beings are able to visually see large portions of their home they call Earth from a distance of 2,000 kilometers in space. For many it is an incredibly awesome experience to be in space inside an enormous organic ship."

Aboard Starship Cosmos these leaders and citizens from Earth are meeting with the high counsel of the IFOP. Among the leaders there is a large contingent of Metaphysicians from earth. They have been invited to join this prestigious meeting by Spiritual Beings of like minds aboard Starship Cosmos."

Looking up at the sky, the BNN announcer interrupted his own report of the meeting to tell his viewers, "If you care to look up at the skies, you can see ships on all sides like a ring around Earth, which of course is exactly what it is."

The broadcaster paused so everyone had time to look up at the sky and then continued, "Now back to the meeting ... ."

All participants have converged in what seems like a very large theatre. It looks to be about 500 meters in diameter having an oval shape. It has theatre-style seating about 50 meters high. It is lit up with thousands of LED lights, in crystal-like chandeliers. A speaker's podium is at the bottom with a panel behind the podium consisting of about thirty seats. This panel is undoubtedly used when the leaders of the Counsel of the Starship and the leaders of Earth's countries are meeting.

Just like after a heavy rainfall, there is an atmosphere of fresh oxygen and negative ions filling the room. The seats are shaped like round cubicles and appear to be suspended in the air. The chairs are very comfortable and somewhat like a large leather office chair with a high back. One arm rest has a small tablet like a computer. The entire cubicle spins around and goes up and down. It is equipped with a large monitor, a microphone and the universal translator which David invented. Yes, that's right. Each participant is equipped with the universal translator."

David, speaking to President Castrorez of the USA in private: "The monumental moment is finally here. Mr. President, Pleiadians have anticipated this moment for a very long time. For most Earth Beings, I'm sure it's a shock beyond description. Please remember that these loving Pleiadians have traveled a very long way for one purpose. That purpose is to respond to thousands of Earth Beings who have asked for help with their understanding of the pros and cons of ascension and whether or not they should choose to remain in the body, in this three-dimensional world."

President Castrorez: "I agree with you David. I

know that as we speak cataclysmic events which began some three years ago all over the world are accelerating exponentially. More than nine hundred million people already have died from massive floods, earthquakes, volcanic eruptions and many other unusual disasters in the past ten months alone. Our world is no longer in denial. Panic, violence and destabilization of many social structures are rapidly increasing. People all over the world are frightened, disillusioned and looking for answers. Then, just like in a Sci-Fi fairytale, suddenly these Beings (Pleiadians) appear out of nowhere with 10,000 huge ships surrounding our planet. At night our sky is lit up like Christmas completely obliterating the stars as we know them. And now this! Hell David, ten minutes ago I was sitting comfortably in the Oval Office having a heated debate with several Republicans about these events. Then I get your call about this meeting and I'm instantly transported to the Pleiadian mother ship Starship Cosmos. It's okay, David. I get it! We are in a twelve-hour count down to the alignment that according to prophecy is predicted to finish us off. Then as quick as a flash I'm standing here looking out this window and what do I see? I see earth for God's sake—surrounded by 10,000 ships. Yes, I realize we were informed of all this several days ago. But teleportation or whatever they call it—that was not expected. Yet, David, teleportation sure beats crowded, noisy aircraft … right? My goodness, the meeting aboard Starship Cosmos is about to start."

Oh! Before we start, David, I want to personally thank you for your caring and hard work. I'm grateful you are one of the good guys."

Captain Elana, of Starship Cosmos to First Mate Sandra: "Are we ready for live broadcast to Earth?"

Sandra: "Yes Sir ... in 60 seconds on channel 01."

Captain to Angelica: "We will be live in fifty seconds and counting."

At the opening of this meeting in about ten seconds ...

Sandra using telepathic communication with David: "Sir, we are live in 3, 2, 1 ... ."

David: "Greetings to all. My name is David. The UN has appointed me as their ambassador for the purpose of this meeting and prestigious event. Welcome to Starship Cosmos: Madam Spokesperson for the Pleiades and The Inter Galactic Federation of Planets, Angelica from the sister Planet Alcona, and your four sisters who are: Sara, from the sister Planet Maia; Teresa, from the sister Planet Electra; Sharia, from the sister planet Astrope; Karen, from the sister planet Merope; Mr. Banatu, President of the UN all of the delegates of Earth Countries and all of the special members of Pleiades and this amazing ship Starship Cosmos. Welcome to all our Brothers and Sisters. The chair will be handled by Angelica, our sister and spokesperson from Pleiades."

0849.23 hours, countdown to Alignment, Omega, the End and Alpha the beginning.

Angelica began this important meeting, "Welcome all Spirit Light Beings, my Brothers and Sisters. We are live on channel 01. Every television, every radio, every ham radio, every commercial electronic means of communication, all cell phones, the Internet and computer tablets on Earth can receive the communication of everyone translated into their own language and dialect. This meeting is one hundred percent transparent. We are all members of the Light Force of Love Energy. There are more than 3,000 channels on our satellite system linked from our orbiting star ships. To my Earth Brothers and Sisters, please go to channel 01, click index and click the first two letters or so of your language; i.e., French click Fr. You will hear and see all the proceedings happening up here on Starship Cosmos. You will hear the proceedings in your own language, for example, if you speak French you will hear the proceedings in French. We will wait a few minutes so all countries, cultures and people will find the channel best suited for their needs."

Please everyone, welcome to Starship Cosmos. I want you to know that we are here from Pleiades representing the Intergalactic Federation of Planets for the following reasons:"

We were invited by thousands of people here on Earth over a long period of time to assist Earth and the Solar system to survive its encounter with the alignment with the Black Hole and its whirling disk at the center of the Galaxy. I know that not all your leading scientists agree with this Alignment and its catastrophic effect on Earth. We are here because what the scientists have told you is true. In less than eight hours your Solar system will go through the whirling disc at the center of the Black Hole. Our Pleiadian descendants (you) are faced with the most important decision of your history."

Every adult of eighteen years and older living on earth will have the opportunity to vote. The votes will be recorded electronically through the internet. A passing vote for the referendum has been set at eighty percent and has been agreed to by both the United Nations and the Pleiadians."

Assuming the referendum passes and is thereby accepted, shortly after Earth will be cloaked with a very powerful shield created by the 10,000 ships you see in the sky. Everyone on Earth will experience a pleasant ride through the Black Hole. Remember, you are our descendants. You will be saved. We love all of you dearly. If the Referendum does not pass, we will leave as quickly as we came."

We are here because Earth is about to undergo a major shift and uplifting of her consciousness. The Pleiadian High Counsel has determined that, unlike previous attempts to colonize Earth that failed miserably, this civilization is worth saving. There is another issue we are all facing shortly; that is, to ascend to the fifth dimension or to remain here in the third dimension physically on this planet. If you choose to ascend you will be required to achieve one single thing: that is to recognize in your heart that you are a Spiritual Being, non-corporeal, having this amazing experience in human form. If you achieve the embodiment of this recognition and believe it in your heart, you will ascend to the fifth dimension. Once in the fifth dimension, you will have a choice to be in your body or not. You may continue to enjoy this incredible planet in your body or you may choose to be elsewhere with or without your body. We Pleiadians of today exist in the fifth, sixth, seventh and eighth dimensions. Sometimes we choose to be in the body and sometimes not."

If more than 20% of you vote no, we will leave immediately and everyone will perish including Earth."

David: "This is the deciding moment of mankind!"

Following David's declaration that this is the deciding moment, many speeches were given from many leaders throughout the world. Many questions were asked about the pros and cons of the assistance from these aliens.

Finally after several hours and emotions running high, Angelica asked for a vote. After all, time was running short.

Much to the delight of most people attending this meeting, the referendum passed with ninety seven percent in favor of the assistance so generously offered by the Pleiadians."

David took a big sigh of relief and then said, "It's interesting to ponder, what would end up being the obvious catastrophic destruction of life if we Earthlings had decided not to accept the help of our Pleiadian ancestors. The thing to remember here is that we always have a choice, and this is the most important lesson here: the concept of volition, the ability and the right to choose between two or more options."

Again David sighed as he silently acknowledged

the end of his musing and said, "Now let's get back to the action. There are less than four hours remaining before our reality becomes something far beyond our imagination. As you can see, people are scrambling to the teleportation platforms where they are being sent back to their families. They want to be with their loved ones as this incredible change takes place."

The vote finished, Angelica regained control of the meeting saying, "By the way, there is one more thing. We will now order our ships in orbit to form a shield. Right before your eyes you can observe our ships in orbit ... all 10,000 of them. They are forming an electromagnetic shield far greater in strength than anything the Black Hole is capable of penetrating and destroying."

As Angelica spoke the sky began to turn into a silver glimmering dome surrounding the earth. It was a sight to behold!

As everyone looked up at this miracle unfolding Angelica said, "As we pass through the Black Hole, this shield will protect Earth from the destructive nature of the incredible electromagnetic forces emanating from the Black Hole."

0200. 00 hours remaining

Angelica has David speak directly to me in my dreams saying, "It seems like a lifetime—to be sure, the longest two hours ever experienced by any human. In spite of the anticipation, the atmosphere present in

186

this room is absolutely electrifying. The energy is so upbeat we can feel a shift happening right before our eyes: from distrust, fear and anxiety to an incredible feeling of oneness."

The inevitable is expected to happen. Earth is expected to pass through the Black Hole. Indeed, the 10,000 ships will provide a protective shield saving Earth from being destroyed by the incredible electromagnetic forces."

With the passing through the Black Hole, Angelica said to expect the following, "After the shift is completed, on Earth all light fifth-dimensional Beings will be able to move freely from this Earth plane in a non corporeal form or remain here on Earth in human form.. Life will be ruled by Love and Universal Law— Love directs the way, and Universal Hunab Ku Law makes the way possible!"

This new globalization will be experienced as the opposite from the fear-based Illuminati-controlled globalization envisioned by the Illuminati before this event. Cooperation will flourish without greed, devoid of the need for accumulation as the sole driving force. In this new world paradigm, the driving force of cooperation will be a genuine caring attitude shared by all its people. This caring cooperation is something few people ever imagined."

Most people will not remember what the world was like prior to the cataclysmic shift; however, they will experience and remember the environmental upheavals like the moon disappearing causing the Earth's axis to shift back to its original way of being as a Light and Love based planet (before the Dark Energy incarnated Earth). This imminent transitional shift will only take six days. Earth's fifth-dimensional reality will be blessed with a very moderate climate with no extreme temperatures. I saved the best for last."

Angelica turned around to spring this incredible surprise on David. She had a twinkle in her eyes as she said to David, "You see, now that everything is said and done regarding the meeting, David, I have a surprise for you!"

David replied, "Good! I like surprises."

With this, Angelica uttered the word, "Energize!"

The room began to glow with a bright white light. They heard the song of *We are Spirit Light Beings*.

We are Spirit Light Beings
Having a wonderful human experience.

We are Spirit Light Beings
Here for a moment in time and space.

We are Spirit Light Beings
Learning to love again.

We are Spirit Light Beings
Walking each other home.
We are Spirit Light Beings

What happened next was nothing short of a

miracle, an incredible expression of love.

Right before their eyes the whole room people witnessed the emergence of a large pool filled with water and two dolphins. Yes two dolphins: Myra and her mate Jona. They leapt and dove in spectacular displays of joy and fun.

Almost simultaneously two more Beings materialized. They were none other than Margaret Chartrand (David's Mother) and Pierre Chartrand (David's father). They both appeared in human form.

The room was electrified with standing ovations, laughter and incredible gratitude'

Wait, is there not something or someone missing?

"Yes, Sandy where are you?" cried David.

He heard a faint voice from nearby. Slowly from behind the pool, the figure of Sandy emerged bathed in bright light. David ran towards Sandy with open arms.

Sandy saw David and ran to him with open arms. They embraced with an outstanding wrap of arms and were silhouetted by the shining white light surrounding the whole group.

Sandy and David met with such force that they lost their balance and fell into the Dolphin pool, much to the delight of Myra and Jona.

First Sandy raised her head above the water and stood. David was swept up by Myra and taken for a fast ride around the pool and then deposited in front of Sandy facing her. David stood and took Sandy's hands in his own and looked deeply into her eyes. Sandy also looks intently into David's eyes. David deliberately and slowly said, "Sandy I love you with all my heart."

Tears formed in Sandy's eyes and she said, "David, I love you with all my heart, now and forever."

David ran his fingers through Sandy's wet hair, gently drew her to him and gave her a tender loving kiss.

As David and Sandy embraced and kissed, gradually the bright light dimmed and the radiant Spirit Beings were showcased in golden Love Energy.

After the magical kiss, the excitement began to quiet down ... .

David turned to Sandy and in deep gratitude said, "I love you, Sweetheart. Thank you!"

The entire World joined in the celebration. People from all over the Globe stood up and applauded. With their applause the meeting on Starship Cosmos finally ended and not too soon because there was only one minute remaining until the alignment.

0001.09, The End is Near; the Beginning is Upon Us

At this meeting there existed an incredible power of Love—so much so that everyone felt overwhelmed.

David proclaimed, "This, my Brothers and Sisters, is the moment! In less than one minute the dimensional shift will be in motion!"

Everyone was wide eyed with anticipation as the seconds counted down.

David continued, "In a matter of ten seconds we will travel through the Black Hole and through the whirling disc. The journey will only take seconds; yet, it will seem like a lifetime. You need not worry about a

single thing. I know the Earth is protected."
9, 8, 7, 6, 5, 4, 3, 2, 1 … .

00:00:00 hours to Alignment, Alignment, The End

The journey through the Black Hole can best be described as a scene from the Stargate SG-1 TV show where the Sg-1 team journeys through the Stargate. Everyone on Earth, the 10,000 ships in orbit and Starship Cosmos experienced going through a hypnotic spiral winding tunnel full of many bright colored lights. The experience seemed like it took a very long time, but in reality it was only about eight seconds. The effect of the journey was profound.

Love was definitely in the air!

+00:00:03 hours, Beginning!

A new dawn, a new day in paradise!

Angelica: "As I speak I am informed of breaking news" (Angelica broke down in tears as she was overwhelmed with the sudden presence of Light, God, Love).

Through her tears of joy Angelica continued, "My Sisters and Brothers from everywhere, I am pleased beyond words to tell you that David has just informed me that we are now on the other side of the Black Hole. Feel the Love energy! To my Sisters and Brothers on Earth, can you feel the awesome difference in you, through you and around you? The negative energy on this planet has been removed. Yes, the alignment is over! The shift has now taken place. Earth is a love based world!"

Half in shock President Castrorez exclaimed, "Oh My! What just happened?"

With hot tears streaking his cheeks, President Castrorez was barely able to speak. He was overwhelmed with a new emotion, an emotion of peace and an obvious absence of stress, fear and distrust. He got up off his chair and took a few steps to where Mr. Hu Jintoa, the president of China, was sitting. President Hu Jintoa saw Castrorez coming and rose to greet him. Castrorez stopped about two meters in front of him. They looked into each other's eyes and with not a word spoken they both advance with arms outstretched. Then the two most powerful leaders (former enemies) embraced with a hug that very quickly becomes contagious. Suddenly every member of every nation started hugging.

David mused to himself, "Five billion Souls here have just experienced the awakening of their Quantum Love Gene. I'm sure they are all watching this happen right on television. We are witnessing a miracle where everyone is waking up from a very long and terrible nightmare. Very few remember the world as it was ten minutes ago."

As the sun rose over the horizon on every television, smart phone and laptop all over the world in every language it was announced that The Quantum Love Gene had awakened. A message was flashed across the horizon.

Dream #40 April 9

Now, I know! The most powerful force in the universe is love!

Love = God/Kunab Ku/Creation Expressing

Dream #41, and Just When I Thought It Was All Over … Yes, One More Dream

Earth Re-Terra Formed

David spoke, "Wow! It is hard to believe. What a truly amazing experience. Seriously, I need your attention, just for a moment. There is another humongous gift that our Ancestors wish to give us. Angelica, would you please announce this yourself."

Angelica announced, "Thank you David," as she gave him a huge hug and a kiss on the cheek. "My fellow Pleiadians, and I do call all Earth people Pleiadians, we have waited thousands of years for this moment. It gives us indescribable joy to present you with this gift: Earth will undergo a *re-terra formation.* That's right! Bless her soul, Earth will return to the magnificent beautiful jewel that she was 2,000 years ago. This will take six days. While waiting, for six days you will be our guests. Yes, that's right! All 5,000,000,000 of you will be teleported to our ships … that's only 500,000 people per ship. Don't worry. We have plenty of room in our 10,000 ships. After the six days have passed, on the seventh day you will be beamed back to your new paradise, Earth"

Those of you who have ascended as of today, you will begin to notice a lot of changes in your body. First you will begin to discover you possess many of the abilities we have: such as telepathy, teleportation, incredible empathy and compassion for all people—Black, Yellow, Red, Brown and White. These changes happen gradually. They will integrate into your Being slowly throughout the next thirty days."

Those of you who have chosen to accept our help but not to ascend will spend six days as our guests also. On the seventh day you will be teleported back to your incredible Paradise. You will experience Earth as it existed in its pristine condition 2,000 years ago. It will be yours to enjoy!" The 13% who voted No will parish.

We Pleiadians will return home to Pleiades as quickly as we came. We are delighted beyond words knowing with absolute certainty that we have done the right thing, and also, that you know you have done a wonderful thing. Welcome to Paradise Earth!"

Back on Paradise Earth, you will notice that the moon is being returned to her home to the dark region of space many million Light years away. This means that the Earth will shift its axis back to vertical; that is, the North and South poles will be perpendicular to the sun. This shift on Earth's axis will usher in the return of moderate temperatures all over the world."

Because of this Polar shift, on the *New Earth* you no longer will require the use of fossil fuels. Oil will be used only to fabricate de-combustible objects. In other words, you will still have plastic to use, only it will also be totally recycled ... no garbage."

How wonderful! I am so appreciative. As I am talking I'm looking at brightly lit auras ... all of yours—marvelous! You seem so delighted. The energy in this room is filled with overflowing love and gratitude."

Angelica was aglow herself as she continued, "Back to telling you about your new life: you will experience no hunger, no pain, no struggle and no enemies.

And as I say these things you have already moved through the Black Hole, you are looking at me strangely and in your thoughts you are saying: 'What is she talking about? Can't Angelica see I'm perfectly happy, loving and peaceful?' Exactly! From this moment on your progress in the arts, science and space travel will parallel your spiritual growth. No longer will progress be eroded by greed, hate, violence, racism and all negative dark energy."

And so it happened. On the seventh day five billion people were beamed back to Earth, to Paradise. Four billion people ascended to a fifth dimension and by choice most decided to remain in their bodies. Five hundred million people did not ascend; however, they do have their beautiful planet back. They are surrounded by ascended Beings, some even friends and family. Living side by side with ascended Beings set them on a quick journey frequently leading to enlightenment and the acceptance of their Quantum Love Gene. Eventually they too will ascend and join their fellow Spirit Beings, as in Truth we are all One.

No sooner did the five billion people reappear on earth, than the sky was lit up with stars (Pleiadian Ships). The stars flashed multicolored beams of light in their final display of good bye wishes and blessings to all Earth Beings for a magnificent life. Then as quickly as they emerged, the flashing stars disappeared into the uncharted darkness of night. What was left behind was a familiar sky filled with familiar stars.

Still in the dream, I say to Angelica, "Wow! This has been an amazing story. Now let me get the message clear. We, Homo Sapiens, are in fact fifth-dimensional Spiritual Beings. We are non-corporeal and enjoying an amazing journey in human form. Is that about it?"

Angelica says, "Yes, that is exactly right! Raymond, I know this movie and book are done in the fifth dimension. The third dimension moves a lot slower. They will manifest. Your job is to keep the faith. Remember what your mentor, Dr. Ernest Holmes said, 'Thoughts become things. And, so it is!'"

Having spoken these words, Angelica disappeared. I slowly pried open my right hand and let the pen drop to the paper. I took a deep breath as I slowly got up from the chair, managed to find my legs, walked over to the bed, and flopped myself down. This time—no dream, well, at least none that I needed to write down in the morning!

THE END